RECEIVED

JUL - 7 2009

By

HAYNER PLD/ALTON SQUARE

HAYNER PUBLIC LIBRARY DISTRICT
ALTON, ILLINOIS

OVERDUES .10 PER DAY MAXIMUM FINE
COST OF BOOKS LOST OR DAMAGED
BOOKS ADDITIONAL $5.00 SERVICE CHARGE

THE SINFUL LIFE OF

Lucy Burns

Elizabeth Leiknes

bancroft
press

Copyright 2009 by Elizabeth Leiknes
All rights reserved.

No part of this book may be reproduced in any form or by electronic means,
including information storage and retrieval systems, without written permission
from the publisher, except by a reviewer, who may quote passages in a review.

All the characters in this book are fictitious, and any resemblance to actual
persons, living or dead, is purely coincidental.

This novel is meant for older readers. It's a morality tale that highlights the ever-present good and evil around us. If you, as a parent or an adult, know an advanced reader (15 and up) who shows interest in the novel, it is, of course, up to you, but it would probably be best if you previewed the book first. —Elizabeth Leiknes, Author, and Bruce L. Bortz, Publisher

Published by Bancroft Press ("Books that enlighten")
P.O. Box 65360, Baltimore, MD 21209
800-637-7377
410-764-1967 (fax)
www.bancroftpress.com

Front Cover Design by Mark Leiknes
Interior Design by Tamira Ci Thayne
Book Jacket Photo by Matt Theilen

ISBN 978-1-890862-62-6
LCCN 2008937343

Printed in the United States of America

First Edition

1 3 5 7 9 10 8 6 4 2

b18725442

For Hardy and Hatcher

Prologue

July 1976

"Your blood looks funny."
"Shut up, Lucy. We're from the same bloodline, retard. Insulting my
blood's like insulting yours.*"*
Ellen and I had read about becoming Blood Sisters in Superteen
Magazine, *so we smudged our combined blood on page 37 and repeated the oath, customizing it to give it some personal flair:*

> I, Ellen/Lucy, promise to be a good Blood Sister (and a
> good Real Sister) by always telling the other if she has
> a booger hanging from her nose, by letting her borrow
> my jeans and/or roller skates at a moment's notice, and
> by doing anything, ANYTHING, necessary to keep her
> from harm.

With one last pinky swear, it was official.
"I promise."
"I promise."

Three months later, the night before my eleventh birthday, Ellen was hit by a big red truck on Highway 71 during our after-dinner bike ride. She died for exactly two minutes, thirty-three seconds, and then was revived.
"Coma."

That word, somehow dirtier than death itself, hung in the sterile air as uniformed people with sorry faces scurried down the hospital hall.

"Honey," my mother said with a forced smile and tearful eyes, "we're staying with your sister while she sleeps. Carol here is going to take you home and stay with you tonight." (Carol was our next door neighbor.)

Later that night, I snuck outside in my flannel nightgown to make a wish in the backyard. A harvest moon flooded the October sky as I tiptoed down the sidewalk, past our big oak to our pretend mailbox, which stuck out of the Indiana soil in front of our playhouse.

We had a real mailbox in the front yard, but this one was for kids. It was a monstrosity of donated parts—a dented, metal body from the Johnsons; a wooden post from Mrs. Clark; and a red signal flag from the abandoned school.

We delivered "Dear Santa" letters every Christmas to our magic mailbox, which transcended space and time. Deep down, I doubted the validity of our special delivery system, but Ellen believed in it. "You never know," she said.

So while she lay in the hospital, I stared in hope at the metal box perched on a crooked post and read my letter one last time.

> To Whom It May Concern:
> I know I've asked for things in the past that I said were really important, but this time I'm not lying. I swear I'll never ask for anything else if you make this one wish come true. Make Ellen wake up and I'll be forever in your debt.
>
> Sincerely,
> Lucy Burns

All I heard that night was wind sweeping through the oak tree branches outside my bedroom window.

I tried to sleep while keeping my fingers crossed.

When I awoke the next morning, I heard my parents in the kitchen telling Carol the incredible news. Ellen had woken in the night asking for two things: butter-brickle ice cream and me.

Mother cried and hugged me tight. "It's a miracle, Lucy. God's given us back our Ellen."

Embarrassed that I'd chosen to put my faith elsewhere, I ran to destroy any evidence of my desperation. I opened the dilapidated mailbox, but the letter was gone. In its place was a small folded note.

Dear Lucy,
    It's a deal. Happy birthday. I'll be in touch.

Sincerely,
"To Whom It May Concern"

Chapter One

I recently turned twenty-nine—again.

When I looked in the mirror that day, I saw my birthday self. My face, youthful in an unexpected way, was dewy-pink and firm. My eyes, bright and clear, lied about how I felt on the inside.

From a chain around my neck hung a silver letter "F," curvy like a Laverne and Shirley monogram. When the light hit, it at first shimmered, then glared. The reflection looking back at me said *beautiful*. It said *perfect*. And I was growing tired of it.

It was three in the afternoon, but I still had my pajamas on—a silk, black, baby-doll chemise, which came to a flirty halt just below my panties. On my feet, I wore my birthday wish from two years ago—Dolce Gabbana's special edition high-heeled slippers for people who have everything. What really sold me on them were three lavender flowers that looked like dainty crystallized iris petals. Five-hundred-and-sixty-dollar shoes can make you feel like a woman no matter what time of day it is.

I love things like sexy shoes and beautiful lingerie now. I didn't always; I used to be awkward, plain. As a kid, I had the same appeal as elevator music—infectious yet unsavory. One on one, people liked me, but I wasn't cool enough for them to admit it in public. Giving me a high-five at a party was the equivalent of getting caught tapping your fingers to a Pat Boone tune or belting out a Neil Sedaka ditty in the shower.

But when He began granting me birthday wishes, I started asking for changes. Over a three-year period, I became a different person, soon possessing a body most girls would die for—tall, mostly legs, and real breasts a normal person would have to buy. And He'd arranged for me to remain young and beautiful—forever.

I was a dream, or that's what I'd been told.

So, on my usual re-birthday, He called for my wish. I asked for Johnny Depp to install my cable—not the 1980s Brat Pack Johnny Depp with the Flock of Seagulls bangs and Viper Room scowl, but the recently oh-so French, pirate Johnny Depp with long silky hair and smart glasses that say "I vote even though I'm married to a super-model."

Then I changed my mind when I thought of another possibility: a sweaty, shirtless Johnny Depp trimming my hedges. So I requested Johnny Depp to be my new lawn boy, but He reminded me of the rule—birthday wishes can't involve anything sexual.

"Complicated," He once said.

I knew what He meant. It would distract me from my work, the job I was groomed for. I was only supposed to attract men, not court them.

So I ended up asking for the return of an old friend I'd abandoned in a thrift store more than a decade earlier. By the time the phone call ended, my friend had arrived—six of him, to be exact. Propped up against the wooden post of my mailbox were six vintage albums featuring the greatest easy-listening pop idol who ever lived—my one and only, Teddy Nightingale.

Teddy Nightingale was his stage name. His real name, Craig Larson, didn't live up to his musical genius, and as I stared at his six albums on my front lawn, I saw him in all his glitz and grandeur, and recognized each album cover right away. The first one featured a colossal-sized Teddy atop a snowy mountain, armed with a clunky, super-shiny microphone. The cardboard cover was faded and had a chewed-off corner thanks to Muffin, our childhood dog. I flipped through the six-gifts-in-one until I found le crème de la crème—Teddy's first live album. And there he was at center stage—a heavenly, spotlighted Teddy looking to the sky with outstretched arms in a perfect purple-and-silver spandex jumpsuit.

I brought all six albums into the house to help me celebrate, and lined them up on my kitchen table next to my chocolate fudge birthday cake. For breakfast, I'd eaten the whole cake, except for one saved piece. Last year's birthday wish was to be able to eat unlimited and varied forms of chocolate, but not gain weight. Chocolate in ridiculous doses is no worse for my ass than a platter of broccoli.

So, as I'd done so many times before, I sat alone in front of a makeshift shrine dedicated to a misunderstood '70s icon. Being with him again was like wearing my oldest sneakers. I made a martini, lit a skinny pink candle, and made a secret wish.

I fondly remembered past birthdays when my whole family was in attendance. Since college, I'd spent all my birthdays alone, but a birthday never seemed like a birthday without my sister (and blood buddy) Ellen. For lots of reasons, both complicated and painful, I wasn't supposed to have Ellen's family life. I was married to my work.

I hadn't seen Ellen for over twenty years.

I missed her.

After my solo birthday party, I replaced the Tony Bennett CD with a Teddy Nightingale record. I'd never gotten used to the modern technology. CDs are just mini-records, but what I most hate about them is how perfectly boring they are—shiny, compact, indestructible, crystal clear. One of the most beautiful sounds in the world is the static-crackle that accompanies a vinyl record—even one that skips is cherished. It's a sign that it's played a lot, and loved.

I fired up my computer for the day, but was interrupted by four deliberate knocks.

"It's the police."

I took another sip of my drink, put on my slippers, and took one last glance at my computer screen. *Your numbers are down.* The software program keeps track of such things.

It usually took me a few seconds to figure out if my visitors were simply random guests, or if they were there because of my job. I turned the volume down on Teddy and went to see what type of company I'd be dealing with.

I tucked my hair behind my ears as I always do when I'm curious, and approached the peephole in my front door. It was a crisp October afternoon, almost dusk. The leaves had completed their transformation from lush green to fiery orange, which reminded me I needed to rake my lawn, and the cold air slapped my exposed skin.

Two police officers greeted me when I opened the door. My shiny dark hair cascaded over my shoulders and covered just enough of my breasts to hide my goose bumps.

They both tried not to react when they saw me, but the one on the left stared hard at my thighs. He was the typical sheriff-looking kind—his belt, riding way below his bulging belly, looked like it needed rescuing.

Frank Webster. Right on time.

The average person never would've guessed he was two years behind on child support, or that he regularly molested Jessica Daniels, the eight-year-old girl who lived next door to him, but it was evident to me. I had the special talent of seeing people for who they really were.

It was part of my job.

Frank was restless. He placed his hand on his nightstick as if he might have to use it. *Good luck, Frank.*

The other officer, younger and leaner—"Collins," his name-tag said—was much more relaxed. His dark hair was all messed up from the brisk autumn breeze.

"Afternoon, ma'am," he said. "Are you Lucille Burns?"

"Yes, I'm Lucy Burns." I smiled.

"We're sorry to bother you, ma'am, but we have a few questions. May we come in?" His voice, deep and resonant, matched the rest of him. I imagined a taut, strong body. What a nice surprise.

"Sure. Come in." I turned to the side and invited them into my home. That was always the first step. *Check.*

The cute one ducked his head to avoid hitting the doorframe. They both walked through the threshold and took off their hats.

"Here. Let me take those for you. I'll put them with all the other ones," I laughed.

"No. That's fine," they muttered in unison while looking at what appeared to be a fairly normal house. As good cops should, they took a mental inventory of my belongings. Seeing no obvious signs of illegal activity, they relaxed a little and began to walk around the living room.

The handsome one touched the arm of my couch and absorbed the surroundings. With a curious look in his eye, he thumbed through Dante's *Commedia Divino* and *The Ultimate Baby Name Book*, both of which were sitting on my coffee table.

"You expecting, ma'am?" he asked as he pointed to the baby book.

"No. Wishful thinking."

On the wall directly to the left of the front door was a painting, Fragonard's *The Swing*. A young lady flew through the air on a swing, kicking off her slipper as her lover admired the view from below.

Officer Collins walked over to the painting, then looked at me. "I love this one."

A bit surprised that a cop could appreciate art, I responded, "Quite sensual, don't you think?"

He blushed while his partner, Officer Webster, rolled his eyes. The only art "Fatty" was familiar with were the cartoons in *Jugs*.

"Yeah, *very* sensual. Do you paint?"

"No. But I think it's captivating how so much emotion can come from a simple picture." We walked over to another painting on the wall and left the very nervous Officer Webster by the door. "For example, take this one." We both gazed deep into de Chirico's *Mystery and Melancholy of a Street*, trying to figure out what the other one was going to say.

It was an eerie sight—somber colors, harsh lights, and foreboding shadows. A lone girl shared a deserted square with a gypsy wagon, and a mysterious figure cast a long shadow.

"She's afraid of the shadow," he said, then waited for my approval.

"No," I said, shaking my head. "She's not afraid at all. She's oblivious. That's what's so scary."

Officer Webster, annoyed at the attention Officer Collins was paying me, looked at his watch. "Miss Burns," he said, "we're here because the police department has some concerns about the amount of thermal energy being emitted from your home."

"Thermal *what*?!" I had feigned the same ignorance many times before.

"Yes, ma'am. Heat. We're talking about heat coming from your house."

"Since when does generating an absurd amount of heat qualify as a crime, Officer?" I asked with a smirk.

"Well, ma'am, with all due respect, it qualifies as a crime if you also happen to be using high-powered lamps and growing enough marijuana in your house to supply all of northern Nevada."

"Marijuana!" I cackled, then repeated "marijuana" in a softer voice and pulled back the curtain to see if the nosy neighbors across the street were observing the police visit. "I don't know the first thing about marijuana."

I moved forward and touched Officer Collins's arm. As I gripped it, my talon-like nails caught skin. He knew he should remove my hand, but instead, much to his own surprise, he allowed me to keep touching him, and felt the need to explain his arrival at my residence.

"Sometimes the heat sensors in the helicopter are inaccurate." A pause. "Maybe there's been a mistake."

His partner raised his eyebrows. "Mistake? Officer Collins, can I talk to you a minute?"

Officer Collins ignored him.

"Wow. That's a new one," I said. "Since when do helicopters have heat sensors?"

"Just procedure, ma'am," Officer Collins explained, smiling and fidgeting with his hands. Considering he was a follow-the-rules kind of guy, it was bizarre behavior, but there was something special about me and he knew it.

I mesmerized him.

He extended his hand. "I'm sorry I didn't introduce myself. I'm Officer Collins. You can call me John. This is my partner, Officer Webster."

By now, Frank Webster was feeling out of sorts, and I began to see the telltale signs. Nervousness. Flushed face. Sweating. That paranoid look of impending doom. Yep, he was the one, all right.

He was a caged rat trying to find an escape route. His chubby, hairy fingers fondled his belt buckle because he didn't know what to do with his nervous energy. It's funny how they always try to control the situation. This guy, for instance, was trying to hurry up, so he could get out of the house. But you can't outsmart fate. It just doesn't work that way.

"Jesus Christ, it's a hundred degrees in here," he said under his breath. "She must have one damn big furnace."

I whispered, "The biggest, Frank."

Officer Webster grew pale, but Officer Collins remained unsuspecting. "You'll have to excuse my partner, here. He's just a little edgy today. Ma'am, I think we'd better go ahead and do what we came here to do. Let you get on with your day."

He looked at Frank Webster, who was now drenched in sweat. "You check the basement, Frank. Why don't I take a look around up here?

And then we'd better get back to the station."

"Good idea!" I said. "Come with me, Frank." I walked him over to the basement door, put one arm around his shoulder, and placed my other hand on his arm, squeezing it and winking.

He stared at the basement door. He was surprised to see it, and rightly so. Basements are rare in Nevada. Something about the water table. The door was enormous, and resembled one from sixteenth century Spain. Unlike the other doors in the house, this one was a giant slab of oak hung on black iron hinges, and it did not open or close easily. Right in front of the door stood my chocolate labrador, Pluto. He sniffed Officer Webster's pant leg, then moved out of his way. Frank Webster looked to me for help, but there would be no rescue.

I delivered the bad news. "He's funny about strangers. Guess he's giving you the go-ahead, Frank."

Frank Webster took his first step down the stairs. When his right leg started to shake in uncontrollable spasms, he stopped. He turned his head around to see me standing next to Pluto, who was now more beast than dog.

I continued to control him. "Go on, Frank."

The shaking of his leg ceased, and Frank proceeded down.

One step.

Two.

Three.

"Is this . . ."

"Yes, Frank."

From above, I gave him one last scorching look and shut the door. *Check.*

Relieved, I skipped back to the living room to talk with my new friend. Officer Collins walked around the room, making eye contact with everything but me. I continued to follow him, mimicking his every move like a shadow. Little did he know that while he was checking my house for drug paraphernalia, I was imagining what it would be like to seduce him right there in the living room. I followed so closely behind him that, when he turned around, he smacked right into me. My slippers slid on the hardwood floor, and with great momentum I crashed, almost hitting my head on the coffee table.

It took me a moment to realize he had a direct view of my thigh and sheer black panties. *Perfect.*

"All right?" he asked with an embarrassed chuckle. He crouched down and held out his hand—half-tentative, half-excited. When he helped me to my feet, our eyes locked. At that very moment, he felt the urge to go check on his partner, but I held him in place. He could not take his eyes off me. He knew he should behave like a professional, but I took away his ability to be rational.

He broke the tension. "Do you work out of your home?"

"Yes." I sat down on the couch and motioned for him to sit next to me.

He sat down and peered into my eyes. "What exactly do you do?"

"I'm in . . . personnel."

"Do you own your own business, or do you have a boss like the rest of us poor souls?"

"Got a boss, and he's a real devil. Took me nine years to get promoted."

"Been working my ass off to make detective but feel like I'm getting nowhere," he said. He moved closer.

"Well, my boss has such a giant operation going, he gets bogged down with all his employees. It's my job to keep track of all the comings and goings."

John Collins leaned forward. "Sounds like you have a lot of responsibility."

I smiled, and when I took one of his big hands in mine, I explained how much I was enjoying his visit. It had been forever since I'd had a visitor like him—a man worth my interest. I took in all of him. His sweet, boyish smile coupled with his strong, masculine body highlighted what he really was—a fine specimen of a man capable of helping me create benevolent and beautiful offspring. Averting my eyes for a moment, I spotted *The Ultimate Baby Name Book* on my coffee table, and I was reminded of my true goal. A peaceful, contented warmth consumed me when I thought of loving and protecting a child of my own.

I now ran my tongue over my lips, and he moved in closer. I made no attempt to tease him. It had been too long.

His warm hand reached the bottom of my chemise, so he slowly walked his fingers across the silk. Our breathing became louder, slower, synchronized. In a one-handed swipe, he enclosed both of my wrists in a tight grip, then lifted them above my head. With my arms held hostage, his lips and his free arm moved in for further investigation.

He smelled like Altoids and chocolate, and it made me want to eat his tongue. John Collins was the birthday present I'd forgotten I wanted. *Arrest me. Arrest me. Oh, God, please arrest me.*

And then my body began to tremble. This time, the focus was less about desire and more about purpose.

His touch was both gentle and confident, and it made me want to follow him. Taking baby steps together, we inched our way toward the couch, but during the excitement, we knocked over the vase of red Gerber daisies on my sideboard. The water seemed to trickle onto the floor in slow motion, or maybe we were moving in fast forward.

Either way, I found myself easing up on the mind control, which was a mistake. There was something about the way he touched my hair and called me Lucy that made me let down my guard.

Just when I did, we both heard a scream from the basement. John Collins broke his gaze and jumped up. "What was that?" he said, reaching for his pants. "Frank!" he yelled.

I sighed and followed him over to the basement door. Blocking the doorway, I wondered if I'd be able to diffuse the moment that was to come. Pluto let out a fierce growl and tugged at Officer Collins's pant leg. "See? Pluto doesn't want you to go down there, either."

"Ma'am! Step away!" He pushed me back into the kitchen.

I felt nauseated.

"It's not your place to help," I insisted. "There's nothing you can do for him. I have strict orders to only let certain people down there, and you're not one of them!"

I'd barely finished my sentence before he flung the door open and was halfway down the stairs. John Collins disappeared in darkness and all I heard were screams, which were strong at first and then got quieter with each second. I shut the door and puked in my kitchen sink.

"Shit."

Pouring myself another martini, I went back into my office to re-open the appropriate file. The program would update the numbers, but I needed to document the specifics. It was part of my job.

I typed in the technical details about the two cops, and then felt compelled to add a couple of pages expressing my feelings about the cute one. I knew it wouldn't be appreciated. I was a mere facilitator.

October 11, 3:42 p.m.

One—Frank Webster. Status: Expected.

I paused for a moment, feeling a wave of guilt and disappointment.

Two—John Collins. Status: Unexpected.

Chapter Two

Officer Collins was the first innocent I'd lost and, in retrospect, that accident got me thinking I might want to quit my job. What may have bugged me most was the fact that his unintended demise didn't bug me enough. Even taking into account the guilty ones, my nagging conscience was the reason I got my car washed so frequently.

I should explain. It was soon after I moved to Reno that I started frequenting the Snow White Car Wash. The first time I went, it was for practical reasons. My car was dirty. I felt dirty.

Somewhere between the baptismal pre-wash soak and the spot-free finish, though, I noticed I felt lighter, more relaxed and, like my car, cleaner. With my tires locked on the metal track, the car inched forward, and on every third mini-lurch, I turned to witness my dirtiest parts, gurgling in defiance, sweeping down, down, down the drain.

Near the end of the cycle, I caught a glimpse of my new self in a large mirror hung near the car wash exit. It was hazy and out-of-focus, but it was me.

Squeaky himself completed the ritual. His real name was Ken, but his buddies called him Squeaky. He was a little person, so he collected my money from atop an old bar stool in the graveled driveway where he wiped down cars and whistled "Whistle While You Work."

Squeaky owned fourteen different-colored T-shirts that made his tiny biceps look big, but they all said the same thing: "Dirt Happens." He never said one word to me, but he looked at me as if he knew I was a good person stuck in a sinful life. Every time we said our silent goodbyes, he would smile at my vintage Camaro, then glance at the sign above his work station that read "Life Is Dirty."

So, when my next-door neighbor Maggie asked me why I washed my car so damn much, I told her about my toxic self. I couldn't talk to her about what I really did for a living—it wasn't allowed—but I told her I was dissatisfied with my life. I was supposed to keep away from the general population, but I was lonely and Maggie was always home. She was my only friend.

What I told people about my occupation varied from week to week. Some thought I was a big corporation bookkeeper. Some thought I was a writer. Others thought I was a personnel coordinator. They were all right. I was a bit of all those things. But nothing good came from what I did, I told Maggie, and I was so far in, I couldn't get out.

"Stop with the drama," she said.

We sat in her skeleton of a kitchen having breakfast one morning after her son had left for school. Her husband David had been remodeling their kitchen. He estimated the job would take two weeks. That was eight months ago.

David's mild-mannered face hid behind a blanket of beard and long brown hair. It was always clean and pulled together, but his edgy appearance didn't match his generous attitude. Their house was in a constant state of upheaval because David was always helping others with *their* projects.

Maggie's mother-in-law called her "Shikse Mags" because she was a Gentile and ate swine on a daily basis. David, who became extra Jewish on special occasions, and especially when his mother visited, liked me because I made his wife laugh.

Maggie was frying ten pounds of bacon and shielding her hand from grease splatters when she said, "Do what you want, Lucy. Fuck your job."

Maggie was the only stay-at-home mom I knew who swore like a truck driver. But she had a strange, slightly iridescent light that only I could see. It framed her face and somehow softened her acidic commentary.

And she was smart. I'd once made a comment about how coffee was more addictive than cocaine, and she told me a story about coffee's sinister roots. It turns out some Ethiopian sheep-herder noticed how hyperactive his sheep became when they ate coffee plant berries, so he decided to try them himself. Some passing monks chided him for ingesting the "devil's fruit." Ironically, the monks soon discovered that eating the plant helped them stay awake for prayers. Through time and necessity, the "devil's fruit" evolved into a spiritual tonic capable of clearing foggy brains and inspiring truth.

And so it was for us, too. Whenever Maggie and I weren't drinking coffee, we were downing cocktails. Sometimes we met for an afternoon martini, talked about what books we were reading, and made fun of the nosy women on our block. But when the school bus arrived, Maggie went into mom mode. "Fresh-baked cookies if you eat your vegetables . . . No television until homework's done . . . Are you making good choices?"

This was her life and I envied it. A sign above her kitchen read, "There are no coincidences," and this is how she lived—deliberately.

One day, she sipped her orange juice and handed me a small box wrapped in yellow construction paper—homemade wrapping paper courtesy of her son Finn. He'd drawn a picture of him and me reading a book, and written, "TO LUCY, FROM THE HOFFMANS," with a brick-red crayon.

A string of excuses trailed from Maggie's mouth. "It's probably a stupid gift. You might already have it. But I saw those albums by your mailbox yesterday."

She put her glass down and folded her arms, unsure if she should give it to me. "I thought it might be perfectly retro, you know, so . . ."

I opened it and smiled when I saw the initials U.S.N.

"Very heady, Maggie. I'm impressed." I couldn't help but hug her.

"I love it."

It was an obscure double-album called *The United States of Nightingale* featuring fifty original songs by Teddy. Each song was a narrative poem celebrating a different state. The album was Teddy's tribute to the highlights of each state of the union, from Alabama to Wisconsin. I was familiar with the songs, but I didn't own the album, and it was the kindest thing anyone had done for me in years. I teared up while telling her thank you.

Once I gained my composure, I told her I was going to begin each day by singing "Nothing Could Be Sadda Than Leaving Sweet Nevada" and not to laugh if she heard me crooning in the shower tomorrow morning.

On my way out, she added, "Oh, I almost forgot. I need a teensy favor." When she said *teensy*, she scrunched her face up and pressed her thumb and index finger together.

She wanted to know if I'd host some dumb girlie party at my house the next evening.

"You know I hate that stuff," I protested. "God, did you know Amway is one of the most prevalent cults in America?"

"It's not Amway," she said when I shook my head. "And no, it's not Tupperware." She grabbed my hand and averted her eyes, knowing I was going to give her endless shit. "It's Pampered Chef." Before I could articulate my rebuttal, she was already making her case. "I promised Sarah I'd have it, but David has the kitchen in a shambles with the remodel, and besides, it would do you good to have some people over. It'll be cool, Lucy. We'll put a real pagan Halloween slant on everything—get everybody into costumes and rile up the girls on the block."

She eventually wore me down and I agreed to be a party hostess this one time. I'd begun to depend on Maggie, and I respected her versatility. One minute she was driving a powder-blue minivan complete with the "My Kid Is An Honor Student" bumper sticker, the next minute she was planning absurd parties just to promote neighborhood camaraderie, and capping it all off as a martini-drinking potty mouth who, deep down, feared being normal.

I spent the afternoon thinking about Maggie's penchant for persuasiveness, and about Teddy Nightingale's album. It wasn't flag-waving patriotism, the kind you see on bumper stickers with buff bald eagles ready to kick foreign ass; it was honest and lovely, the kind of songwriting that made me want to take a coast-to-coast road trip and stop at every diner in between.

"If You're Lucky, You'll Land in Kentucky."

"We're in Missouri, What's Your Hurry?"

"How I Found Rapture in New Hampshire."

Teddy's lyrics somehow sneaked their way into people's subconsciouses, into their souls. A crowbar couldn't remove "Held Up in Arizona with My Beautiful Ramona."

Some call Teddy Nightingale the musical antichrist, but those are the same people who sing along to "I'm Well Aware That My Heart Resides in Delaware."

I was thinking of my favorite resident and good neighbor Maggie when I was reminded of a conversation I had two weeks ago with Finn. I babysat him while Maggie and David went to the movies.

I had just tucked him in when he asked me to read his birthday page again. Every time I babysat, I read to him from *The Magic of Birthdays Book*, a giant compilation of personality profiles for each day of the year.

"Okay. It says about your birthday, 'You don't like boring relationships because of the influence of Uranus on your life.'"

"The influence of my anus?"

I love seven year olds. "No, Finn. Uranus. It's a planet."

"Like Mars?"

"Yeah," I said, putting my hand on his. "Okay. Your birthday is January 11th. The number one is ruled by the Sun and so, in your situation, you have double power." He looked at me with little-boy pride, and I smiled at him.

"It says many people born on the eleventh possess a special calling to 'help the world in a time of transition.'" He stared hard at the page, trying to figure out his responsibilities.

"What's transition?"

"It means change."

As he crawled into my lap, he said, "Keep reading, please."

I wanted to, but as I silently scanned ahead to the next paragraph, I saw things I didn't want him to hear. "Concentrate on the idea that you are alone. At certain times in your life, you'll need to walk your path without anyone by your side. By accepting this destiny, you will become strong and receive inner strength and knowledge."

No child should have to sacrifice himself to walk any path alone.

"Is that the end? What am I supposed to do for the world when it changes?"

"Nothing, sweetheart. Just be happy." I tucked him in. "Time for bed, Finnster."

"Aren't we gonna say prayers?"

"Do you say prayers every night?"

He was excited. "Yep." I was surprised. He helped me put my hands together, and we bowed our heads.

"I go first. God bless Mom, Dad, Grandma and Grandpa Mills, Grandma Hoffman, Dylan, and Rusty. Please make Ryan's sister get better, and help Mom take care of everybody."

We sat in silence, heads still bowed.

"It's your turn, Lucy," he whispered.

It was the longest we'd ever been quiet together. I hadn't said prayers since before my sister had her accident.

"Um, thank you for my health and my family. Amen."

Finn looked at me, skeptical. "You have to say their names."

I started to feel sweaty. My work situation had forced me to give up my family a long time ago, but I wondered where they were, if they were still alive. "Bless my parents." I looked at Finn. "Bless your mom and dad, and Ellen."

"Who's Ellen?"

"My older sister."

"You have a big sister? Why doesn't she ever come to your house?"

How could I answer that? Let's see, because if she did, she'd discover my secret, and then she'd die? *Sweet dreams.*

"She lives really far away, and it's hard for her to get here."

"Oh." He thought for a moment. "Maybe Mom could help her get here. Maybe she could—"

I placed my finger on his lips. "No, Finn. I'm afraid that won't work. But thanks."

He snuggled under his blanket. "Hey, if God lives in heaven, and he can do anything, why does the book say it's my job to help the world?"

"Sometimes it takes just one person, Finn, to make a difference." Sounding like a first-grade teacher, I was terrified at what I might say next.

"Maybe God can't hear us when we pray. Do you think he can?"

I knew I had to be genuine on this one, or he'd be on to me, so I told the truth. "I do."

"How do you know he can?"

"Faith, I guess."

"What's faith?"

I sighed. "Hmmm. Believing in something you can't see."

In a matter-of-fact tone, he admitted, "I believe," and he yawned as he laid down his head.

And I thought of Ellen, and how she believed in our pretend mail-box, and in good triumphing over evil.

I turned off Finn's bedroom light and closed his door.

"Lucy?" his voice called out from the darkness.

"Yes?" I opened the door just a little.

"I forgot to ask God to bless *you*, Lucy." Light seeped through the cracked door, and I could've stood there forever.

Then, as he pulled his covers over his head, I heard an embarrassed Finn taunt me. "And God bless your boyfriend, too!"

I whispered back, "I don't have a boyfriend."

"I know. Mom says you need one."

Giggles filled the room.

Chapter Three

January 1977

I*t had been five months since Ellen's accident. Teddy Nightingale topped the charts with "Sunrise," and life in Alliance, Indiana was like a new day.*

I had forgotten about the note-in-the-mailbox incident—I was just thankful to have Ellen back. She was in eighth grade, I was in seventh, and we retreated to the places we cherished. An elaborate blanket tent in the walk-in closet, a pretend bunker in the cellar, an elaborate tree house in the big oak—this was our realm.

Upstairs in the bedroom we shared, I buried myself in the stuffed animals she kept propped up to perfection on our bed. Cracks of light shined through a sea of plastic-eared dogs she'd won at the Spencer Fair and a variety of teddy bears from boys she no longer liked.

"Be happy with what God gave you," she'd always say to me when I complained about my looks.

I changed the subject. "Ell, do you believe in heaven and hell?"

I'd attended church for the final time on a sultry Sunday the previous August. It wasn't a popular idea—my quitting church. After all, it was Indiana, the heartland of all things pure, and a place where people don't quit anything. The late '70s were especially difficult for farmers, yet so many of them came to our little church every Sunday, wearing their best Levi's, driving freshly washed Chevy's, and looking for hope. But I wasn't a farmer—I was just a girl.

The sermon that day was one I'd never forget. "What does the world need?" asked Pastor Ovard. Before anyone could think about it, he went on to answer his own rhetorical question, "Well, it's not the love that Dionne Warwick refers to in her song."

I felt like a traitor. The very song he mentioned rang out in a quiet metallic twang every time I opened my jewelry box. The pastor went on to assure us the Beatles were wrong, too, when they sang, "All You Need Is Love."

Would God really damn the Beatles to hell?

Maybe John.

I was confused.

Then the pastor lowered the boom. Apparently, love was not a bad thing, but it wasn't the only thing. "What we truly need," he said, then pausing and looking out into the congregation, "is forgiveness."

Later that night, when Ellen and I were playing Scrabble, *I asked her the question I'd been thinking about for a long time. "Seriously, Ell, what do you think happens to us when we die? Who's to say which sins are forgivable and which ones aren't? I mean, do you think heaven and hell are really that far apart?"*

For eight points, she added a "d" to my word "save" and said, "My little sister, the sinner. Look, bad seed, is this about you quitting church?" She squished her pillow under her head. "Because Mother will get over it eventually."

It was true—she'd have to get over it. Other girls went to church. I listened to Teddy Nightingale. He was my hope, my religion. While everyone else bowed down to the holy trinity, I spent Sunday mornings lighting candles at my solo shrine to Teddy.

Redemption meant dancing around my room to "Boogie With a Capital B," followed by a healthy dose of intellectual stimulation: Who really did "Sing to Your Soul" anyway?

Teddy's psalms cast no judgments. They provided pure schmaltzy joy. I sang his praises every Sunday, because with Teddy, it was never over. With Teddy, there would always be another song.

Chapter Four

If I was going to host a Halloween party against my will, I was at least going to wear a killer costume.

So I went to the mall.

Everywhere I went, I saw posters for the two movies then duking it out at the box office, *Adoring JC* and *Absolutely Adolf: What Were You Thinking?*

Separately, each movie was typical cinematic storytelling, but side by side, they became a circus sideshow. *Adoring JC* chronicled the last few weeks of Jesus Christ's life, while *Absolutely Adolf* examined Hitler's adolescent years. Each film peddled its own theme-related promotional products at every checkout stand. It was pure marketing genius. At the bookstore, jewel-studded *Adoring JC* bookmarks sold alongside pocket-sized copies of *Hitler for Dummies*.

A teen accessories boutique spotlighted Jesus headbands and Hitler charm bracelets in two towering display cases. At the music store, there were two T-shirts. One featured a Robert Plant-esque Jesus clad in oppressively tight white pants straddling the Stairway to Heaven. The other showed a pimple-faced, punk-band Hitler wielding angry black drum sticks above the slogan, "Beat to your own drum."

But the real contest was happening next to the Halloween store, where a giant line of moviegoers was stationed in front of the theater. Two ushers, one dressed in a Hitler costume, the other as Jesus, and both with matching over-sized boxing gloves, danced around each other in a makeshift boxing ring. Hitler jabbed and Jesus ducked. Jesus threw a right hook and Hitler took one in the jaw.

I left before a winner emerged.

After I fell asleep that night, my photo album resting directly beside me, Teddy Nightingale saved me from drowning. In my dream, I was engulfed in a river eddy. Teddy threw me a makeshift life-preserver—a blown-up toy piano, with a lasso-style rope tied around it. And like a disco cowboy against a backdrop of stars, he guided me to shore.

The next morning, exhausted from my night of dreams, I ingested extra strong coffee and made an attempt to decorate for the party. Onto the kitchen table I threw a black cat serving dish (of the plastic variety) full of candy corn, then duct-taped a cardboard witch to the front door.

After I fed Pluto, I checked my e-mail and was unhappy with what I saw.

Lucy:

Your entries are getting too involved.

No more superfluous descriptions and misguided metaphors. It's simple bookkeeping. Just the facts.

Sincerely,
To Whom It May Concern

He rarely e-mailed. He was old school—preferred snail mail and the venerable mailbox, maybe for old time's sake.

After I finished my third cup of Colombian Dark Roast, Maggie came over to remind me I wasn't fulfilling my potential, and that was ultimately the reason I was unhappy. Then she handed me a book with a thousand dog-eared pages, and a cover that oozed with self-help psychobabble.

"*What Color Is Your Parachute?* Come on, Maggie."

"It looks cheesy, but it's got this aptitude test," she said, starting to laugh. "I'm serious, Lucy. It might steer you in the right direction."

I put the book away, at which point Maggie suggested I take a creative writing class. After finding an unfinished story on my kitchen counter one morning, she knew I dabbled in the literary arts. The real reason she wanted me to take the class, though, was to set me up.

"Come on, Luce, he's smart, sexy, employed, single, and *not* gay. How often does that happen? David knows him from a job he did for the university. I want to introduce you." She mini-punched my shoulder. "I'll bring him by sometime. Maybe you could lose the sexy pajama thing, put on actual clothes, and try to be normal, okay?"

I flipped her off, and she put her arm around me. "Or not."

"Sorry, too busy. Some bitch signed me up to be a friggin' Tupperware goddess, so I have to get ready for this party." I smiled.

"It's not Tupperware," she reminded me. "You're a good neighbor, Lucy."

"Why don't you go home and carve David's face into a jack-o-lantern or something? I'll see you later tonight."

"Lucy?" She stopped at the door.

"Yes?"

"I *am* a bitch, aren't I?"

I threw a handful of candy corn at her as she dove out the doorway.

Chapter Five

My guests were due any time. Other than Maggie, I'd never invited a non-business-related person to my house. It was strange having guests who were actually going to *leave* my house at the end of the evening.

I knew I needed to pretend to fit in, and I was grateful to have a Halloween costume to help with the disguise. Sometime after my third drink—I'd started drinking about noon—the irony of my costume struck me as both comical and depressing. I looked in my full-length mirror and saw everything I wasn't. The black-and-white ensemble accentuated the stark contrast between the life I had and the life I wanted. I twirled around, dizzy from the martinis, and fell onto my bed, but before I could relax, I heard the doorbell ring and, checking the window, saw my first guest.

I stumbled to greet Lindsey Eckhardt—three doors down, country blue and mauve split-level, backyard sprinkled with two jungle gyms and a litany of brightly colored jumbo-plastic Little Tykes slides. The door swung open and there she was, a scarecrow with a housewife's face, crouching down on my porch to pick up errant straw dropping from her pleated denim overalls.

She wore a smile and a frown at the same time. "Oh, what a funny costume, Lucy. A pregnant nun. It's like an . . . oxymoron, right?"

Answering her would just promote discussion, so I silently let her in. I considered singing "If I Only Had a Brain," but she'd either be clueless or offended.

"Wanna see the rest of the house?" I started the tour without waiting for an answer. We went to the kitchen first.

"What's that noise?"

Loud, strange growls and panting came from behind the basement door, which was closed with six heavy padlocks.

"Oh, just my dog, Pluto."

She looked confused.

"Still being house-trained," I said with a shrug.

After the tour, I sat her down on my couch and tried to figure out what someone like Lindsey Eckhardt might want to drink.

My college girlfriends and I used to play this game every Friday night. *What's Their Poison?* we called it. Like construction workers rating innocent female passersby, but more discreet, we wrote our commentaries on little bar napkins. In the beginning, our descriptions were rudimentary—a nice guy was a "Corona," a slutty girl was a "Sex on the Beach."

But over the years, we honed our skills and grew competitive in our drive to mix clever language with fresh and accurate descriptions. A hot guy was a "Dewar's On the Rocks," a lush was a "Vat of Mad Dog 20/20 Mixed in a Rubbermaid Garbage Can," and a sappy sweet girl with no sense of humor was either a "White Zin" or a "Peach Bartles & James Wine Cooler," depending on how annoying she was.

I decided Lindsey was maybe a "Strawberry Daiquiri (Light on the Rum, If You Would)," or worse, a plain old "Apple Cider, But It's Got to Be Organic, Please."

"Shot of tequila, but only if it's Cuervo." Lindsey put her hand on my arm. "*Please.*"

And so it was true. Never judge a housewife by her Halloween costume. I brought us each a salt shaker, a lime wedge, and a generous shot.

"José, meet Lindsey," I said, handing her the shot.

As she pounded it, she grimaced slightly. "What are we listening to?

Neil Diamond?"

Ouch! Spoke too soon. *Sorry, Teddy.*

The rest of the guests arrived shortly after.

Dana Andrews—colonial four-bedroom, still had her letterman's jacket from high school, and owned more than three thousand holiday decorations. Probably a "Chardonnay."

Sara Hopkins—ranch-style home four houses down, cookies from scratch, loved JC Penney's *Home Magazine.* Definitely a "White Zin."

The rest of the women were a cocktail of domestic perfection: an interior decorator, an arts and crafts coordinator, two kindergarten teachers, a handful from the Pilates, Yoga, and Chocolate Support Group, two from the Women as Warriors Book Club, and one cranky church organist dressed up, I thought, as Tammy Faye Bakker.

And then there was Maggie. Dressed as a she-devil, she seemed intent on protecting me from the other women by stabbing them with her plastic pitchfork if they asked me too many questions or exhibited even the slightest condescension.

Kristin Waller started in with numerous, annoying hand gestures. "My daughter Ashley always asks me why you stay locked up in your house like a —" and Maggie swooshed in with demon-like speed and stared her down. Kristin hesitated, but then moved in for the kill. "She thought for sure you'd be a witch for Halloween, Lucy."

Maggie put her arm around her. "So, Kristin, did everything work out with Ashley?" Then she began to whisper, "You know, the trouble at school?"

It worked. Kristin Waller fake-smiled and walked away. It turned out that her daughter Ashley had been caught making out, behind the lunch room dumpster, with a not-on-the-honor-roll boy.

When the Pampered Chef sales lady rang her little bell, all the women took their seats in my living room. I sat next to Sara Hopkins because she made room for me, and because I thought I might stumble over my own drunken feet if I went any farther. We watched one demonstration of a gadget that turned ordinary bread slices into tiny pita pockets, and all the women went bonkers with the thought of making miniature pita sandwiches for their children. There were oohs and aahs from the super-homemakers as they fondled every new kitchen tool that followed. Each of the women boasted of domestic bliss and confirmed her need to be what the party promised: a pampered chef.

"Yes, I've used one of those before," Kristin insisted.

Another chimed in, "I don't know what I did before the Perfect Pancake Dropper. Honestly, my pancakes were ghastly." She put her hand over her mouth.

Everyone nodded.

"The kids kept asking me if they were supposed to be shaped like farm animals or something, but they were just misshapen spectacles."

Sara Hopkins noticed I was unable to join in the excitement.

"Making kids' lunches isn't as sexy as they're making it out to be," she said quietly. "It can be a real pain in the ass."

I was comforted by her attempt to make me feel included, so I asked her about her new baby.

"He's so beautiful. I have such a crush on him. And I feel so lucky. I mean, just looking at Karen makes me feel guilty."

I was confused. Sara pointed to Karen Lowry and Olivia Jakes, who were talking with one another in my kitchen. Karen, fidgety and pale, stood in front of my basement door. "The poor woman has had three children die," Sara said, "each before they were even six months old, and not one doctor could tell her what happened. Thank God they're trying again. It's so damn horrible."

"It really is," I said. I instantly knew just how horrible it was.

Over the noise of the party, I barely heard the doorbell ring. It was the first installment of the neighborhood trick-or-treaters—every arrival a new disguise to figure out. Wands, guns, fairy wings, and capes were clues to each mystery. Who were these costumed little people? I opened the door to see pried-open bags and outstretched arms belonging to pint-sized statues frozen in the flickering light of my angry jack-o-lantern.

They kept coming in pairs, sometimes threesomes, happy to abandon their real personas for the evening. I wondered if the wee firemen really wanted to fight fires when they grew up, and if the lacy princesses recognized themselves in the mirror.

I was getting drunker.

The party was still alive, and Maggie waved at me from across the room to signal its success, but two martinis and several trick-or-treaters later, I misplaced the assorted mini-candy bars and, by mistake, grabbed a bowl from the Pampered Chef lady's party display.

At eight o'clock, Britney Spears and Christina Aguilera, who, I might add, were much too old to be trick-or-treating, scoffed when I gave them a handful of brown apple slices left over from the Super Colossal Apple Slicer demo.

The heavily glittered girls were accompanied by two teenage boys, both pirates for the evening. One of them pushed the other toward me, and said, "Go on, Ricky. Tell her. Tell her she's the hottest piece of ass on the block."

I started to slur my words, but everything that came out of my mouth sounded profound to me. From the safety of my doorway, and over the din of soccer moms armed with checkbooks, I hollered, "Little pirate perverts!"

The trick-or-treaters turned around, shook their rejected pirate heads, and threw the apple slices onto my front lawn. And then I overheard what would send me into the downward spiral that would be talked about on our block for months.

Christina said to Britney, "She's the one my mom was talking about." She shoved a popcorn ball in her mouth, but I could make out a few things in between the mumbling. The words hung in the autumn air, thick as the smell of burning leaves that drifted over from the

Andrews' backyard.

"Bitchy . . . No kids . . . Old maid."

It was a glimpse of my future delivered by two naughty pirates and their wannabe girlfriends.

I struggled to remember what it was like to be normal. Alone on my front porch, I looked down the block, lit by streetlights and silhouetted by black tree branches swaying with increasing intensity. An army of sugar-high children cloaked in various combinations of satin, plastic, and masks marched from house to house, reminding me of a family life I'd never have. And despite my lack of candy, they kept coming. Waves of disappointed witches and cowboys left empty-handed while the real moms sat in my living room buying cake-decoration kits and whatever else helped "make food fun again."

I walked back into the house, waded through the loud chatter of "What are you buying?" and "Jack is going to kill me for spending this much" and ended up in the kitchen, making myself yet another drink. Karen Lowry grabbed her coat and Olivia followed her. Two images of Karen Lowry danced in the air, and when they became one, we made eye contact.

"Karen, you leaving already?" I asked as she blurred by.

Karen Lowry left without saying goodbye to me. I didn't expect her to. She didn't understand the tension, but I did, even in my drunken stupor. Karen would soon become another number on my computer screen. My job had finally intertwined with my real life, or at least it would soon. How was I going to pull that one off?

In a fit of hopelessness, one more drink turned into five and I was soon stumbling around with three Super Colossal Apple Slicers tucked under my arm. An irritated Pampered Chef lady scurried after me. In pure passive-aggressive tones, she raised her voice, "The hostess typically gets only one free gift, ma'am. Ma'am!"

When things turned for the worse, we came full circle—back to the living room. The whole room stopped admiring the goods, and now looked at a train wreck of a situation: me, Mrs. Pampered Chef, and Maggie in a Mexican standoff armed with mouths (and a pitchfork) instead of guns, and a couch of respectable women caught in the middle.

And then came the point of no return.

"Fuck off, Tupperware bitch!" I said as drunken slobber oozed down my chin.

Thirteen jaws dropped in disbelief.

"Lucy, shut up and sit down right now," Maggie said in her most deliberate, serious, and proper way.

The couch, the guests, the order forms—everything started to spin in unison.

"I gotta pee," I slurred, and then asked several guests where my own bathroom was.

They pointed down my hallway, but help had already arrived. Teddy appeared in a flash of pure white light to show me the way. But somehow I went in the wrong direction. I crawled over to the closet by my front door, squatted, and urinated all over my rented nun's habit and Dana Andrews' new Dansko clogs.

The next thing I remembered, someone—a very attractive man, actually—was standing above me.

Maggie had no choice but to introduce us.

"Lucy, meet Luke Marshall. He teaches writing at the university."

And like a good neighbor, I passed out.

Chapter Six

It was ten in the morning before my hangover-induced headache woke me up. "Sunrise" from Teddy's *You're the Light* album was programmed as my alarm, and it had been on repeat since 9 a.m. It wasn't long before horrifying flashes of the previous night's escapades worsened my already throbbing head. When I closed my eyes, each disturbing recollection replayed candid images of me, the worst person in the history of bad people, dancing around like a fool, harassing small children, and pissing on myself, my rented costume, and my neighbor's shoes.

The cheeriness of the song, coupled with my strong self-disgust, made me throw up. This time I found my bathroom. The song's shrieking chorus followed me to the toilet. I couldn't take anymore, so I shuffled out to the kitchen in my crumpled, smelly nun's habit.

I had company, I discovered—Maggie, wearing her coat over her purple flannel pajamas and slippers.

"I heard your prayer, Sister Lucille. Coffee's on the way." She smirked at me, but I wasn't in the mood.

She tried to justify her visit: "The door was unlocked."

I sat down, groaned, and rested my aching head on the kitchen table, while Pluto snuggled at my feet. When he wasn't working, he was droopy and needy.

"I'm sorry I made you have that miserable party," she said, grinding the hazelnut coffee beans.

I covered my ears. There was silence for a good minute before I lifted my head and attempted a smile.

Maggie stared at the dripping coffee, and I knew she thought it was funny—serving the *devil's* drink to a hung-over nun. "If it's any consolation, I don't think he saw your yoo-hoo . . . maybe just your bare thighs, and a little pee running down."

"Sweet Jesus." I buried my face in my hands.

She tried not to laugh. "Come on now, it could've been worse."

"How?! How *could* it have been worse?"

She thought for a second, then exploded with a loud cackle, her eyes filling with tears. "I have no idea."

Her laugh-cry lasted the entire length of the brew cycle. She finally sighed and handed me my coffee. "Well, he said maybe he could meet you another time, so—"

"Oh, shoot me now." I grabbed her arm. "He doesn't want to see me. For God's sake, I peed in my hall closet! Sure, Maggie, I bet he said to himself, 'That's a real hot babe. She loves to host Tupperware parties, ridicule the nunnery, and get so fucking drunk she pees on herself. I gotta get me some of that.'"

Maggie resumed her belly laughing.

"Seriously. What kind of weirdo sees that and wants a date? He's probably a serial killer. Oh, crap, I know what it is," I said, walking over to the coffee pot. "He's into the whole golden shower thing. He's a dirty pee lover."

"He wants to see you." Maggie smiled.

"You are fucking kidding. Why?"

"Because he didn't see you the first time."

I was now thoroughly confused.

"Lucy, he's blind."

I sought clarification. "Blind? Meaning can't-see blind?"

"Exactly. Anyway, I guess you'll find out what he's like. You're meeting him for—"

"If you say I'm meeting him for drinks, Maggie, I swear to God—"

"Coffee. You're meeting him for coffee at the Java House. Sunday. Unless, of course," she said, crossing herself on her chest, "you'll be at church, Sister Lucy."

"Maggie, you're a certifiable bitch. I'm NOT seeing him!"

"And he's not *seeing* you."

I sat in the Java House and looked for a blind man. There was a red-headed lady by the door punching the keys on her laptop, mouthing "shit" every third word. She was drinking green tea. Thankful she'd avoided the triple shot espresso, I wondered if the antioxidants would really prolong her miserable life.

Two college-age kids with impeccable posture sat on a red velvet couch. They must have been on a first date, because they were laughing at inappropriate moments in their conversation. I overheard the boy tell the girl about his roommate, who was recently diagnosed with testicular cancer. She laughed so hard she spilled her drink. When he didn't laugh with her, she started gulping her vanilla latté, then began talking about her cat named Mocha.

"She's adorable, but when I see 'frozen mocha' on a menu," she said, "it makes me think of her." For a split second, she awkwardly mimed a cat licking its paws. "My petite black kitty, frozen solid, topped with whipped cream and cinnamon."

He didn't laugh. Instead, he looked at her like she was crazy. Her latté was gone, so she stared into the empty cup, afraid to look up.

I ordered my own latté and, reminded how important first impressions are, thought about bolting out of the coffee shop. I'd had every intention of not showing up to meet Luke. After all, I wasn't allowed to get involved with him anyway. There was no rational reason for showing up. But there I was, in my favorite shoes, after an hour of primping, secretly hoping he was normal—secretly hoping he would like me.

I approached the unapproachable goth-girl at the register.

"Excuse me," I said. She barked back. And I mean really barked, like a dog. Everyone in line yawned as if this was acceptable behavior. I asked the guy behind me, "Is 'Dog' the standard vernacular for this place?" but he just growled at me, too.

Her multiple piercings must have made her extra hostile, because right when I got her attention, she slammed down a mini stainless-steel pitcher of steamed milk, spilled some on her hand, and yelled "Motherfucker!" loud enough for everyone to hear.

I preferred the dog-speak.

I tried again. "I'm, uh, waiting for someone. I was wondering . . ."

She rolled her eyes and made a hand gesture for me to wrap it up, like on award shows when the winner is talking too long at the podium.

I got nervous and started talking gibberish. "I was wondering if he'd, um, checked in?"

She folded her twenty-something arms, flared her nostrils, and gave me a snotty fake-smile. "Yeah, he just *checked in*. The Penthouse Suite. Or was it the Presidential? Oh, wait." Then she threw her arms up. "This is a coffee shop, not the goddamned Four Seasons!" she shouted.

I started hiving out like I do when I'm humiliated and angry. A big welt formed on my jaw line and started creeping up my cheek.

And then a voice from the back of the line said, "Actually, I *am* checking in late. Sorry, Lucy."

Before I turned around, I took a few seconds to lick the lipstick off my teeth, which ironically he couldn't see, and to generate some self-confidence. Thirsty and under-caffeinated people shooed us out of line. "Hi. You must be Luke."

"I must be." He was confident and sexy, and I was a jackass. *Again.*

Luke was more attractive than I'd hazily remembered. He was tall, like me, and very muscular—not like a big-necked wrestler, but in a lean lifeguard kind of way. He managed to be pretty and rugged at the same time. His "I just woke up" sandy blonde hair looked more sandy than blonde, and his stubble went beyond a five-o'clock shadow. The anti-Ken doll thing worked for him—and for me.

What was in his hand confirmed what I'd thought: He didn't see himself as a victim. His walking cane, which should've been a depressing reminder of his blindness, was adorned with red-and-white stripes. When people saw his candy cane swinging through the air, they probably looked relieved, not sad.

"I wasn't sure you'd recognize me," I said, presenting a semi-spastic hand gesture near my head.

"Your smell." He pointed to his nose and smiled a mouthful of shiny white teeth. "José Cuervo and urine."

I blushed and then extended my hand. "Let's start all over. I'm Lucy Burns."

And so we met again.

After several refills and two hours of conversation, we ended up talking about our college transcripts. When I told him the most embarrassing thing on mine was a series of W's, indicating my bad habit of withdrawing from classes like Advanced Latin and Muscular-Skeletal Biology, he seemed skeptical.

He leaned back in his chair, trying to look aloof. "Sounds like a commitment problem to me."

I wanted him to be wrong.

Chapter Seven

Maggie and I sat at her half-finished kitchen island as I told her how Luke had asked me to audit his creative writing class.

"It's not like a date or anything—it's just for fun," I explained.

Maggie picked at a loose, green ceramic tile awaiting the application of grout. "Get a clue, Lucy. It's a date. Why are you being so weird about this? You're a grown woman. He's gorgeous. He likes you. Get *on* him."

But what she didn't and couldn't understand was that it was an impossible situation—my dating someone. I'd tried this kind of thing before, and it always turned out disastrously. But he *was* beautiful. Maybe just one class.

Maggie swung her legs to the side of the bar stool and told me she had good news, then handed me an envelope. "Early Christmas present. Can you believe it? Front row!"

Teddy Nightingale was going to perform at the Pompeii and we were going. I hadn't seen him in concert since I was ten.

I hugged her. "Oh my God, you rule! He's irresistible! You'll see."

When I stared at his name on the ticket, it made me a little sad that Teddy had been reduced to performing at a local casino. By the end of the '70s, things started to go downhill for Teddy, as if he woke up one day and just wasn't cool anymore. The '80s were a time of excess, and Teddy Nightingale became excessively unpopular. He seemed to respond by preparing himself and his lyrics with extra cheese.

In 1981, Teddy released an album that posed the question, *Should*

I Love Again? and all the critics said, "No, you shouldn't." Their love affair with the king of schmaltz was over. But in the '70s, he'd been electric. He'd churned out number-one hits, song after song. He was unstoppable.

Chapter Eight

October 1977

October had arrived and it was once again my birthday. Ellen and I had finished eating my speckled angel-food birthday cake and were enmeshed in a game of Twister when the phone rang. It was for me.

"Hello?"

"Happy birthday, Lucy." Silence.

"Brad, stop making your voice sound like that. You're such a dork."

"Brad Williams is fishing with his Uncle Ted. As a matter of fact, as we speak, he is catching his first rainbow trout." His voice was serious.

"This isn't Brad."

"Okay, Brad, I mean Mr. Very Mysterious, make this fast. I'm beating my sister at Twister." Ellen was contorted into a painful-looking stance on red and yellow dots. I made a goofy face, pointed to the receiver, and asked, "What do you want?"

"What is your birthday wish this year? You get one."

"Come on, Brad. I know your voice. It's very nice of you to call, but I'll see you tomorrow in Algebra. Bring me a Mars bar or something," I said, laughing.

Again, silence.

"Not hanging up 'til I make a wish, huh? Okay, I want that new backpack from the mall. No, wait," I said, loud enough for Ellen to hear, "I want to look like one of Charlie's Angels. You know . . . flowing hair, long legs, pretty much the perfect body. Oh, and I want Heather Johnson to be jealous of me."

He said, "Is that it?"

"You're really a trip, Brad. I gotta go." Just as I was about to hang up, he spoke again.

"Don't tell anyone about me. Ever. She's only here because of me."

I looked at Ellen, who had abandoned the game and was standing in her cutoffs by the countertop eating her nightly cinnamon-sugar toast. "Who is this?" My smile was gone. "You're creeping me out, Brad."

"I'll be in touch." Dial tone.

Though Brad denied calling, I assumed he was lying and never told anyone about the mysterious phone call. Meanwhile, the next year was the best of my life. My boobs finally grew—proof, in my mind, that I could will my body to do what I wanted. "Firm ripe melons" was how post-puberty-ized breasts were referred to in a book I'd checked out from the library, and I got to unveil mine in the locker room after Phys Ed one day.

Nurse Shirley made a random visit to check all the girls for scoliosis. "Curvature of the spine," she explained, while fifteen girls lined up completely naked from the waist up, slowly bending over in a diving pose. "Bend all the way over so I can see your whole back. You don't want to wear an ugly old back brace, do you?"

I didn't. Plus, for once, I wasn't dreading the mass disrobing of girls with breasts bigger than mine.

Heather Johnson giggled to Tanya Richter, next to her in line, "I wonder if Lucy has on that little girl undershirt like she wore last year."

Last year had been a disaster. As the nurse got ready to examine us, each girl, one by one, tossed her bra into a big pile on the locker room floor. It was a sight any boy in our class would have donated a month's lunch money to see. The very objects of desire they'd dreamt of touching lay there in a flesh-heated mound ready to ignite in pure hor-

mone-saturated glory. Some girls threw in really big bras that had thick mom-like straps. One was beige and another powder blue, but most were crisp and virgin-white, untouched by shiny, still-tight hooks.

None of them looked like what I tossed in. I tried to hide it behind my back, but Heather publicly urged me not to be a party-pooper. So, on top of all of the real bras landed my cotton spaghetti-strapped undershirt featuring the pink satin rose that adorned the scoop neck. It screamed "FRAUD" next to its authentic, mature contemporaries and, all eyes on me, I stood alone and exposed.

But the following year, when it was time to get dressed, I gathered my hand-me-down bra and shook my new additions into place. Not only did they fill out the cups, they stood up in a perky salute, heaving out the top. I lifted my head to catch Heather Johnson, mouth agape, glaring at my newly acquired friends. She quickly looked away, but I was a force to be reckoned with and she knew it. I had arrived.

The year got even better. I grew three inches sometime between Thanksgiving and spring. Baby fat disappeared and my legs rivaled Farrah Fawcett's in her shortest short-shorts. My hair got darker and darker until finally the mousy brown tone turned silky jet black. I got the lead in our school production of South Pacific *on the same day James Berkland asked me out for a dipped cone at Coney Corner. And just as Teddy evolved from a restrained background singer into a full-fledged, larger-than-life pop star, I abandoned my role as wallflower for my new status in the spotlight.*

Middle school eventually became high school, where my transformation became complete. Ellen, the only one who kept me grounded, had gone off to college, and I impetuously decided I was too good even for Teddy. On a Saturday morning, I ditched all his albums and posters at our thrift store, not even waiting long enough to get a receipt. He'd been there for me all along, acting as my secret sentimental side, my spiritual counselor of kitsch and disco. But I no longer found refuge in his voice. The '80s were rapidly approaching and his "The Music's In

Me" attitude wasn't enough for me anymore. I didn't want to be music. I wanted to be sex.

Teddy would achieve no more top-charting hits. The mainstream was falling out of love with his naïveté.

And I was falling out of love with myself, but I just didn't know it yet.

Chapter Nine

October 1984

By my senior year in high school, I looked nothing like the old Lucy, and I chalked it all up to good old-fashioned luck. One year later, on an October afternoon in Bloomington, Indiana, I was studying at the University's main library when I received solid proof to the contrary.

"Happy Birthday, Lucy."

I turned to see who it was. In her country club suit and perfect make-up, the woman was very attractive—a could-be Miss USA contestant. Everything about her was perfect. I could almost hear country music when she opened her mouth.

"Do I know you?" I asked.

"Our boss has been communicating with you for the last eight years. Notes. Phone calls . . . Anyhew," she sighed, "you're finally ready."

"Ready for what?"

"Don't fight this, Lucy. I know you remember." She handed me a folded note.

> Dear Lucy,
> It's a deal. Happy Birthday. I'll be in touch.
> Sincerely,
> "To Whom It May Concern"

I tried to rip it away, but it was no use. She had me. She drove me to Hilltop Park, and we walked until the rolling hills spilled into the Athens Cemetery. The bleak October sky made the tombstones look more ominous, and I got colder as she laid out my obligations.

At one point, while she was standing alone, I ran as fast as I could to get away. But running against hurricane force wind, I got nowhere.

Exhausted, I fell to the ground. She appeared in front of me. "The GM doesn't like it when people don't fulfill the terms of their contract." Her eyes widened, and she added, "You've been enjoying the benefits of your relationship with the GM thus far, and—"

I interrupted. "Benefits?"

"Oh, please, Lucy. Do you think your genetic code intended for you to end up with high cheekbones and the perkiest tits on the block? Do you think James Berkland asked you out in the eighth grade because of your personality? And how do you think you earned a perfect score on the SAT?"

She went on to tell me I was now a "facilitator"—she used to be one, she said. Now she worked out of Branson as a pharmaceutical sales rep, and "supervised" in her spare time.

I had a wicked headache and began tuning her out.

"Anyhew, you'll be pretty much dealing with me. He only deals with the gifts, birthday wishes, and, uh, any problems that may arise."

She noticed my disinterest.

"Lucy? Did you hear me? This is important information."

I'd had enough. "I'm leaving now. Please tell your boss, the little General Whatever, that I don't want any part of this. I never did."

"That's not a good idea, Lucy."

"Look, I'm leaving now. I'm going home and I'm going to forget this whole thing ever happened."

And I did.

For eleven hours.

Chapter Ten

The morning after I ran away from my supervisor, I got a call from my mother. She was crying.

"Lucy?"

"What's the matter, Mom?"

I could barely understand her. "Lucy, you need to come home."

After I got there, we went straight to the hospital. I was terrified to enter the room, but I walked in and tried to be positive.

"Ellen?" I put her hand in mine. In an instant, my eyes filled with tears. I didn't want her to see my fear, so I turned my head and pretended to cough. I barely recognized her. She'd broken an arm, both legs, and several bones in her face. Both of her blue eyes were so badly swollen she could only tell who was in the room by our voices.

"Lucy, is that you?" she whispered.

"It's me. You're going to be fine, Ell. I promise."

The word was she'd been mugged at a rest stop on her way home to visit our parents. I stayed with her for the next week. Late one evening, when Ellen was asleep, the nurse said I had a phone call.

"Mom?"

There was silence. "Now are you ready to fulfill your contract?"

Alone at the nurse's desk, I found myself yelling into the receiver, "If you hurt her again, you lousy piece of shit." I started to cry in desperation.

"Next time, she won't be this lucky. Do you understand, Lucy? He's not fucking around. After all, she should already be dead. He's the only *one keeping her alive.*"

When I woke up, I was wearing a heavy necklace with an ornate silver "F" pendant hanging from it. All the facilitators had one, I was told. To me, it stood for everything but "Facilitator." "Fucker." "Fuck your life up." "Fucking ridiculous." And then there was the aptest adjective of all: "Fucked."

That day in the hospital was the last time I ever saw my family. To keep them safe, I realized I had to start my new life alone. At first, it was unbearable. My mother called every day, trying to figure out why I was cutting her off, and even showed up at my apartment to see if I'd been abducted into a cult or something.

But it was too late. I'd already moved and left no forwarding address. She and Ellen continued to look for me, off and on for the next few years, but to no avail. I couldn't be found. I didn't want to be found.

It was the '80s, and I dressed the part. Each morning, I scoured my room for as many layers of clothing as I could find, put them all on, then topped off the ensemble with dozens of lacy headbands tied around my heavily hair-sprayed head. I sang along with my new idol Madonna, who had, for a time, replaced my once beloved Teddy Nightingale.

I listened to "Papa Don't Preach" instead of "Sunrise" now, but I didn't have a mama, let alone a papa anymore. All I had was a middle-aged drug-peddling succubus supervisor who seemed to be there every time I turned around, and a boss who gave me great birthday presents, but who could also destroy my family any time He wanted.

In between throwing parties, pretending to go to class, and hiding from my family, I worked, but not the kind of consistent work my friends did, like waiting tables or selling clothes. My supervisor gave *me "assignments" that varied from week to week. Every Sunday night she'd call.*

"Lucy, this week it's Todd Wilson. He'll be picking out a new release at Videoland USA on Burlington Street at 8:00 on Wednesday night. As usual, show him the way."

"Okay," I replied, as I always did.

This is how it was. Sometimes I'd be in the middle of a girls' night out, and I'd have to sneak away to complete an assignment. But I always came through. I didn't want to find out what would happen if I didn't.

Sometimes I'd complain about how depressed I was. My supervisor kept telling me how I just needed to go shopping and get laid—not necessarily in that order.

But that was the problem. I was getting laid more than Madonna, but each time, soon after consummating the deed, I'd puke my guts out. Such a reaction doesn't lend itself well to relationships, and this was by design.

Sometimes it was the way he buttoned his pants or the tone of his voice that set me off. One time, to attempt being normal, I went out for coffee afterward, but it ended with my future ex-lover licking his lips the wrong way, and me puking up a double shot of espresso all over the ladies' room floor.

So, of all my fondest birthday wishes, the one I couldn't be granted was a real boyfriend—the kind you see more than once. At first, I thought I was going through a finicky phase, but when I'd slept with every single boy in my Classical and Biblical Lit class and couldn't stand to sit next to any of them afterward, I got suspicious.

"I have a problem." I explained to my supervisor what had happened with Mark, this cute boy who laughed at all my jokes and let me drive his motorcycle. We had four dates, but the second I slept with him, I couldn't stand the sight of him. Everything he did repulsed me—his clothes, his smell, the way he brushed his teeth.

She sighed. "Lucy, Lucy, Lucy. What kind of job do you think you'd do if you had a boyfriend to spend time with—one who, I might add, would ask all sorts of questions about your work? That, my dear," she said, putting her arm around me, "would be a real problem."

"So, I'm not allowed to have a boyfriend?" I said in an even tone.

"Our definitions of 'boyfriend' seem to differ."

I got more aggressive. "I want someone I can—"

My whining irritated her, and she interrupted by grabbing my wrist. "Listen. You can fuck anyone you want, but you can't date them, and you can't have a relationship with them. He designed it that way." She let go, and gave me an insincere smile. "Relationships are overrated anyway."

So, with my long legs and stone-washed minis, I continued to be sex personified. I even slept with a few clients who were on their way out. I figured they'd be the best partners—no complications. But as the '80s came to a close, my big hair shrunk right along with my ego, and I began to feel like a one-dimensional version of my former self. I'd become a beautiful woman wearing beautiful clothes driving a beautiful car. I was Lucy, the cardboard cutout. And there was no end in sight. For my college graduation present, my supervisor bought me the perfect house, with the perfect basement, on the perfect dead-end street—in Reno, Nevada.

I'd be the only facilitator in the city, which meant a big raise. There was no use stewing about it. I couldn't say no.

As I packed, I placed Madonna under a pile of Mrs. Pac-Man playing cards, fishnet tights, and several videos starring Molly Ringwald. It had been years since I'd abandoned Teddy in a pawn shop in Alliance, Indiana, and I missed him. On the way to my new home, I turned on the radio and was reunited with my old friend.

He sang about another girl.

His Sarah was selfless. She gave all of her pure heart and asked for *nothing in return.*

It was a simple lyric speaking the cold truth. I was not Sarah. I wasn't a giver—I was a taker. During the car ride, I tried hard to think of just one thing I looked forward to—one thing I was proud of.

Two thousand miles later, I was still thinking.

Chapter Eleven

After meeting downtown at the Pompeii, Maggie, Finn, and I headed straight for Vesuvius Village, the casino's indoor theme park where Teddy would be performing. We passed horse-drawn carriages, concession stands supported by Roman columns, and scores of brick ovens that commemorated the Pompeiians' affinity for bread baking. Smells of rotisserie meats, wafting through the walkways, made us all hungry for sausage on a stick.

When we got to the Odeon, a small amphitheatre, we noticed they'd created a makeshift gladiator ring for our modern-day cinematic rivals—*Adoring JC* and *Absolutely Adolf: What Were You Thinking?*

Hung on the ring's inside wall was a giant billboard that simultaneously celebrated the two warring movies *and* Teddy's upcoming concert. One half of the board featured a '70s-inspired, jumpsuited Jesus playing the piano and singing, "If you like Teddy Nightingale, you'll love *Adoring JC*." The other half showed Hitler, Teddy Nightingale, and Dick Clark as hosts of *American Bandstand*, boasting, "We give *Absolutely Adolf* an 85 because it has a good beat and you can dance to it!"

In the center of the ring, two men faced off. One carried a staff in his left hand and tucked a loaf of bread under his right arm, his long hair scrunched up under his helmet. The other wore a German officer's uniform under his armor. A moustache was Superglued to the front of his protective face plate, and a swastika to the back. We couldn't stay for the battle, so we continued down the path to the main attraction at the center of Vesuvius Village—a three-story volcano in an open-air courtyard.

They'd built Teddy's stage in the shape of an oozing shelf of lava at the volcano's base. I explained to Finn that the lava part was a bit inaccurate, because the real Mt. Vesuvius had erupted in a Plinian explosion, the kind where a plume of ash and rocks, not lava, smothered everything in its path.

"Don't they make it blow up every hour?" Finn asked.

They did. At the top of every hour, the volcano puked out thousands of Pompeii Bucks (casino coupons that could be used to buy various things in Vesuvius Village) in order to demonstrate what the original Pompeiians hadn't believed—that Mt. Vesuvius was, in fact, alive.

When the time was right, frenzied gamblers scooped up Pompeii Bucks and stuffed them in their pockets. The open courtyard actually grew dark for two minutes every hour until all the Pompeii Bucks settled on the casino floor.

Finn picked one up and gave it to me.

"Thanks, Finnster. Should we get a pig on a stick?"

He smiled. "No. Keep it for later."

While Finn and I took our front-row seats and waited for Teddy to take the stage, Maggie ran off to the bathroom, and the story of Mt. Vesuvius squawked out of the massive speakers.

"The poor people of Pompeii never had a chance," I said.

Finn looked confused. "Why didn't they just leave?"

"Well, according to Pliny the Younger—"

Finn interrupted. "The *Younger*? Who was he younger *than*?"

"His father, Pliny the Elder, silly."

He nodded in fake understanding.

"According to Pliny the Younger," I continued, "most of the people in Pompeii thought the mountain was peaceful, even though it was always on the verge of exploding."

Then Finn pointed to it. "Hey, we should ride that!"

The Bestia roller coaster consisted of thirteen cars, each painted with red and orange flames. It spiraled up Mt. Vesuvius, then down the back side into the Porta Abyssus, a long tunnel through darkness.

"Sure, babe." I handed him another giraffe animal cookie from a little bag of treats I'd packed for him. There was a long silence. Finn looked at me for a moment, as if to say something, but then hung his head.

"What's wrong, Finn?"

"Nothing."

When I looked at him, I knew it was definitely *something*. "Come on, tell me."

"I'm afraid to tell you. You're gonna think I'm a bad person."

I gave him a smirk and handed him a Teddy Nightingale pencil I'd bought for him on the way in.

"Okay. There's this kid, Justin. He rides my bus and I don't like him. I mean, I *didn't* like him."

"Why don't you—didn't you—like him? Is he mean to you?"

"No. That's the thing. He's really nice. To everybody." He frowned, and his voice turned angry, as if he was about to justify something. "It's just that he's good at *everything*. He can throw the football farther than anybody. He never strikes out. And he's the smartest kid in school."

"And?"

"And so last Friday, during recess, I wished he would go away. And now he's gone."

"Finn!" I grabbed his wrist.

He looked at my angry grasp and was ashamed. "I know it was bad—"

"Finn, never, ever wish for things like that."

"I know. 'Be careful what you wish for.' That's what Mom always says." He suddenly looked grown up. "I did it, didn't I? I made him go away."

I took a deep breath. "Of course not. Everybody has bad thoughts now and again. You're human, just like the rest of us."

He didn't believe me.

Maggie came back just as the opening act took the stage and the lights dimmed. I recognized them from their numerous appearances on Dick Clark, *Soul Train,* and *Merv Griffin.* Underneath a sign saying "America's Sweethearts of Soul," Peaches and Herb, facing each other, performed a six-song set of the '60s and '70s soul hits that made them famous. Ellen and I had played their 8-tracks at our slumber parties, and we both had Peaches and Herb dolls. One of my friends even named her poodle Peaches, and made it wear this orange chiffon doggie-dress.

Peaches and Herb ended their act with what we all wanted: "Reunited." The crowd swayed with the melody, and it felt so good, hearing that familiar song from long ago.

The next reunion felt even better. After a few minutes of whispering, the crowd roared when Teddy walked back into my life. Seeing him in jeans and a blazer was such a departure from his album covers—they'd always featured him in flashy jumpsuits—but he looked good. He opened with "Sunrise," and the crowd went wild.

But shortly after he finished his first number, something strange happened. He made eye contact with me. The front row was only a few feet from where he sat at his baby grand, and I looked around to see if he was looking at someone else.

Maggie grabbed my shoulder and sang along. "He's singin' to you, kid!"

He *was* singing to me. During the second chorus of "You're the Light," he left his piano and walked to the edge of the stage. Still crooning, he stared at me with a slight eyebrow raise. In-between lines, he mouthed, "Do I know you?" and subtly pointed at me. No one noticed but me. I looked behind me, but he did it again. What could I say? I knew him—I'd known him my whole life—but he didn't know me. How could he?

He made several more trips to our part of the front row before the end of the concert. Each time he gave me a bizarre look.

Maggie put her arm around me. "We're sure getting our money's worth, aren't we?"

During his very loud finale, "Boogie with a Capital B," I hollered in Maggie's ear. "Did you arrange all this for me?"

"I bought the tickets, didn't I?"

"No, I mean," I said, widening my eyes, "Teddy coming over here, singing to us. I swear to God he's acting like he knows me."

"Yes, Lucy," she said, "I called up Teddy Nightingale and said, 'Teddy, my girlfriend thinks you're the cat's meow. Now be a doll and give her some extra special attention.' "

When Teddy left the stage, Maggie hugged me, wished me "Merry Christmas," and took Finn home. I got in line for the bathroom. As I waited, I looked at a giant poster showing Teddy in a rocking chair reading *What Color Is Your Parachute?*, and underneath the picture it said, "Read! Everybody's Doin' It!"

The horror! I shut my eyes. Is this what had become of him? Doing public service announcements that employed subtle sexual innuendoes to appeal to illiterate teens? And what was it with that goddamned book? Had everybody in the world read it except me?

Just then a woman approached me. "Ma'am, could you please come with me?"

"Is this about where I parked? Shit, I always park in the wrong place . . ."

She frowned as if I had already wasted an hour of her time. "No, ma'am. I'm one of Teddy Nightingale's *personal assistants*. He told me to intercept you before you left." This very blonde personal assistant wore a pink parka, pink hat, and pink gloves, all perhaps to cover up a less than pink personality. "He'd like to see you—if it's convenient."

Convenient? When was it not convenient to chat with Teddy Nightingale? On the way to his dressing room, I tried to act as if this was normal, having a rendezvous with a childhood icon at the local casino.

"Is this your first time meeting Mr. Nightingale?"

I nodded. The hallway was decorated with Teddy's old album covers, all in poster-sized frames and hung in chronological order. Teddy's first dollar ever made was mounted inside a shadow box, and placed between *Sunrise* and *Greatest Hits II*. The door to his dressing room featured one giant blue star with a sparkling gold center.

When I walked in, his back was to me. I looked around for a *Candid Camera* crew. The pink assistant brought him some Chai tea, and Teddy told her we needed a moment alone. Unless a camera crew came in to save me, I would have to speak.

"I'm probably your biggest fan," I started, "but I never was part of any dorky fan clubs or anything, so, I mean, not that fan clubs are dorky, but, I, um—"

"Hi, Lucy." He turned around with a very calm look on his face. His skin had a healthy glow. His blue eyes were clear and calm.

"Um, hi?" I gave a confused smile.

"You're wondering how I know your name," he said. "Well, as it happens, I was once in your line of work."

Chapter Twelve

I couldn't help but snicker. "I doubt it, Mr. Nightingale."

"What do you doubt?" Teddy stood up from his chair and walked over to me. "That I could do what you do?"

I shook my head. "Trust me. You don't have it in you."

But he was certain. "Yep. I'm definitely getting the vibe. Once you're a facilitator, you develop a knack for picking it up in others." He stared at my chest. "And there's the necklace. The GM's making them out of cheaper stuff now, I see."

Suddenly, I felt faint. *Teddy Nightingale* was a facilitator? Teddy freakin' Nightingale?! The excessive Zen-ness of the room didn't help. The smell of incense was overwhelming, and the loud trickling sound coming from several water fountains made me want to pee. *Teddy Nightingale?!*

"This is a lot for you to digest, I know, but I saw you tonight, and you looked unhappy with your situation." He sat back down in his dressing chair and took a bite from his Powerbar. "Am I right?"

I looked bewildered. "Are you? Unhappy with *your* situation?" I asked.

He folded his hands. "Oh, I quit that life a long time ago."

It would have been strange enough talking with the greatest easy listening artist of all-time, but I couldn't believe what we were talking about at that very moment. Years ago, if someone would've told me I'd get to meet Teddy Nightingale, I'd have developed a list of questions regarding his career that went like this:

1. Is it true that your song "Sarah" was originally called "Farrah," but another song with that name came out first that year and you had to change the title and chorus?
2. When you wrote "Boogie with a Capital B," were you really debating Boogie's status as a proper noun?
3. Did you ever consider pulling a Hillary Rodham Clinton or a John Cougar Mellancamp—going back to your original name, Craig Thomas Larson—when you got famous?

However, my current predicament called for questions more relevant to the situation, like, "How did such a nice guy like you get wrapped up in such a bad career choice?" And most importantly, "How in the hell did you get out of it?"

"Lucy, I don't have much time, so let me get right down to business. I know what you're going through. Been there, done that. Since you're a big fan, I want to help you." We stared at each other. "How long have you been *under contract?*"

I took a deep breath, and told my idol what I'd never told anybody. "From what I can figure," I said, "I sort of committed myself, unwittingly of course, when I was ten. Then in college, things really took off. The next thing I know, I'm living in Reno, controlling the portal to, well . . . you know." I pointed down with both index fingers.

He took a sip of his tea. "You think *your* basement is *the* portal?" He chuckled as only Teddy Nightingale drinking Chai tea could. "You're small cookies, kid. The real portal—the mother of all portals—has an unusually powerful lure." Teddy sighed and stared off into space, as if he was about to share an age-old secret. "The real portal is the Bestia."

"The Bestia?!" I freaked out. It was like having the Almighty himself answer the questions I'd had for decades, so after he explained some of the logistics, I interrupted, "Where are the other portals? How long were you involved? I need to find a way out of this without hurting anyone . . . What about—"

"Hold your horses now."

One of Teddy's personal assistants came in carrying some clothes and set them on the top of the wardrobe. When he saw me, the assistant did a double-take and lingered in the room, straightening up some of Teddy's toiletries.

Unable to control myself, I continued in a loud, desperate whisper, "What about my supervisor? How many are there? Am I really going to be able to see Ellen and my family?" It all exploded, very loudly, with, "Oh, my God, will I be able to have a real boyfriend and have sex without vomiting?"

The assistant looked at me as if he wanted to be the first one in line if the answer was yes. Teddy gave him a disapproving look and he slinked out of the room.

An embarrassed Teddy leaned toward me and spoke, "Don't start your engines just yet." I found it strange that such a progressive Chai drinker had such an extensive collection of odd, old-fashioned phrases, all having something to do with cars or horses.

"I have a question for you," he said. "It is the only question you need to concern yourself with right now."

I swallowed.

"Do you want to be saved, Lucy?"

I had to think about what he was saying. It had been a long time since I'd allowed myself to think I *could* be saved. "Of course I do."

"I ask this because the journey to freedom is very hard. You need to be one hundred percent committed."

"Well, *you* did it, right? You sold yourself, became successful, and then somehow got out of it?"

Teddy Nightingale looked irritated. "Well, let's apply some logic here. Was I once successful?"

"Ridiculously so," I answered.

"And am I now?" he asked with a raised eyebrow.

An honest answer would be rude. "Sort of?"

"You can say it. It doesn't upset me. I will never again regain the kind of success I had thirty years ago, and I don't miss it." I found myself thinking about nightingales—dull, colorless birds that sing sad, sad songs. "Back then," Teddy said, "it was all I dreamt about. You obviously asked for beauty. I asked for talent."

I felt shallow and tried to defend myself. "Actually, I first asked to save my sister. The beauty came after the fact—"

"Anyway, that's how I got involved—I prayed for ten hit songs, and He provided them, only it was the *wrong* He pulling the strings," he said. "By the time I figured it out, I was enjoying my success and afraid what would happen to me if it ended. Long story short, I found a loophole and freed myself, which was great, but my songwriting talent went into the shitter." He shook his head in shame.

"Tell me about the loophole." I needed to know.

"Well, after a lot of research, I discovered a way out—a loophole that consists of completing three big tasks in exchange for total disaffiliation from Him."

He looked behind both his shoulders, lowered his voice, and raised his index finger. "One: You need to accelerate your rate-of-departure success, by a lot. You've gotta help fifty-four clients meet their fate before the due date."

"Fifty-fucking-four!" I blushed knowing I had just cursed in front of a pop idol who was trying to help me.

"Yeah, it's a lot."

"What's the due date?" I said.

"If you ask, He'll give you one. If you can deliver the right number of souls within the designated time frame, along with completing the two other tasks, He'll let you go. If not, well, I'll tell you about that in a second. It's a sick game He plays." He held up another finger. "Two: You need to find someone to replace you as a Facilitator."

"Like who?" My mind raced.

"Doesn't matter. Pick someone you don't like. Three." He held up a third finger. "This is the difficult one. You need to take out a target."

That sounded bad. "What's a target?"

"I don't have time to explain. The name of a target in your local area will be mailed to you, as soon as you complete the first two tasks. Good luck, kid. I gotta go." He shook my hand. "They want an encore."

The crowd was still chanting, "Ted-dy! Ted-dy!"

That was it? I had so many more questions. "Wait. Are there more like you? I mean, famous facilitators? Give me one name—I'm dying to know."

He threw back a shot of Chai like it was vodka. "Maury Povich."

I knew it!

On his way out, he said, "One more thing, Lucy. Once you commit to doing these three tasks, there's no turning back."

"Right." A chill tingled through me. "What happens if I don't complete them within the allotted time?"

His face lost expression. "You get transferred to the Main Office. You don't want to go there."

An entourage came in to whisk Teddy Nightingale away. As he shuffled out the door, he said in a quiet voice, "If you ever need help, call me," and he handed me a card with his name and personal phone number printed in a very happy font, and the word "peace" written in fourteen different languages.

Peace—I wondered if I'd ever find it.

Chapter Thirteen

To celebrate the good news Teddy had given me after his concert, I settled into my couch and put on "It's Extraordinary." As always, it skipped right in the middle of the chorus. I had listened to it so many times that even when I heard it on the radio, I anticipated it skipping in that same spot.

There was no question that what he'd told me was extraordinary. Miraculous, really. Just the possibility of getting my life back made me feel genuinely hopeful. I'd almost forgotten what hopeful felt like.

I crouched down and pulled out a white box from underneath my bed. The box was overflowing with envelopes, and lifting it onto my bed made me feel uneasy. I took each envelope out of the box, except the black one—I couldn't bear to open that one.

No one knew my big secret, especially Ellen. A long time ago, she wrote me a letter telling me she didn't understand why I didn't want to see her, and she couldn't handle not being able to communicate with me. She told me she was going to write to me, and sent the letters to a post office box back in Indiana. Maybe it would be like our magic mailbox, she explained—no matter where I was, she could reach me. As it turned out, she was right. I arranged for a fellow Facilitator in Indianapolis to forward her correspondence to me. And Ellen consistently wrote me. Every month.

Until today, her letters lay sealed in a tomb of regret, but now I opened them one at a time. Day turned to night before I got even halfway through. In one day, I lived Ellen's whole life—her college graduation, her first job, her wedding. I pretended I was there for everything—when she got a promotion, when her cat died, when my father got sick.

And then came the "Dear Little Sister" letter I wasn't prepared to see:

> *She's tiny, only seven pounds, but she's the most beautiful thing I've ever seen, and there's a sparkle in her eyes that is new and familiar at the same time. And when I tell her she's named after a very good person, she smiles. Isn't that nuts? I wish you could see her.*
>
> *I miss you more than ever,*
> *Ellen*

I tried to savor each letter after that, as if by slowing down, I could stop time, but I couldn't. Little Lucy got older every time I opened an envelope. I held myself together until the last two letters. As I read the one in the smaller pink envelope, my tears blurred the words, and I had to get a tissue to continue.

> *Thank you, Auntie Lucy, for the awesome leotard. I love the purple stripe. I can finally do gymnastics at the YMCA. Mommy said I couldn't do it until I was eight. She said you were good at front handsprings. I wish you could teach me.*
>
> *Love,*
> *Lucy*

Just as I put the letter down, my doorbell rang. I opened the door to find Olivia Jakes standing on my front step, flowers in hand. The last time I saw her, I was somewhere between my sixth or seventh martini at the infamous Pampered Chef debacle. My head hurt at the very sight of her and her daisies.

I squeaked out an awkward and surprised, "Olivia? Oh, hi."

She flashed a warm smile and handed me the flowers. "Sorry I'm late. This was really nice of you, Lucy. Brunch is my favorite meal!"

Had I turned into Betty Crocker overnight?

"Your invitation was adorable. How on earth did you get the card-stock to look like a bowl of fresh fruit?"

Shocked by her presence, I wondered why she stressed that the fruit on the invitation was *fresh*. Had she seen it done with unfresh fruit before? As I pondered how one might make an invitation in the shape of a fruit bowl, it dawned on me what had happened. My supervisor had sent her the invitation.

There were three ways my supervisor contacted me about clients and homework. The first and most common was by phone. The second was by random client drop-ins, where I had to figure things out for myself. The third, and rarest, was when my cold yet creative supervisor (who liked making homemade paper crafts) would send my client a fancy invitation, usually adorned with embossed ink and beads, and forget to tell me.

At the party, I had apparently been wrong, thinking it was Karen Lowry who had been murdering her children. When I looked at her, it now was clear to me that Olivia Jakes was, in fact, the real sinner involved. At the party, Karen was standing beside Olivia, and I must have transposed the two. I was trained to pick up on strong emotions such as fear and guilt, but sometimes I got confused. It didn't help that I was shit-drunk at the time.

As I looked at Olivia walking around my living room, I saw each child's death. Olivia and Karen were friends, so it was easy for Olivia to get away with the murders. The first baby died during a party that Karen and her husband were throwing. Olivia snuck upstairs and smothered him. The next time, she did the same thing while the baby was napping and Karen was doing laundry in the basement. The third time she poisoned the baby with an untraceable drug—Olivia was a nurse. Karen and her babies weren't her only victims, I saw. Scores of patients had been killed on Olivia's shift.

I walked over to her and took the invitation. After all, it would have to be destroyed. No evidence could be left behind. With help from my supervisor, I could arrange postcards, in Olivia's handwriting, saying goodbye, she'd run off with the gardener and wouldn't be coming back.

"Olivia, how's Karen?" I folded my arms and waited for her to begin showing the telltale signs. I had done this hundreds of times, and though I knew they were absolute evil in the flesh, I still got an ache in the pit of my stomach when I saw their faces.

She became sweaty and pale. "Um, she's fine. Isn't she coming today? The invitation said brunch for seven. I just figured . . ."

"No. She's not coming, Olivia." I shut my eyes for a moment. "You'll be the only one."

"Oh? Oh."

I brought her into the kitchen. Pluto started in with the growling and foaming. Even in this dire scenario, Olivia kept looking around for quiche, juice, and muffins. She really did like brunch. What a pathetic person—she knew her bad deeds had caught up with her, yet she didn't want to go out on an empty stomach. But there would be no brunch—only payback for dirty crimes undetected by the local police.

"Olivia, would you like to see my amazing collection of wine in the basement?"

"I'm not much of a wine drinker," she said, and began crying.

"Right. I'm still gonna have to ask you to go down there."

I finally gave Pluto the signal. I felt like the goth-girl at the coffeehouse. "Yeah, yeah, yeah. No time to listen to you yak."

After disposing of all traces of Olivia, I needed to come clean, so I went to see Squeaky. He gave me the deluxe wash as if he knew I was extra dirty. As always, he was right. The pre-soak barely made a dent in my grit and grime. He sent the jumbo rollers back twice to drown out my badness.

On my way out, I glanced in the mirror, and the reflection was different from last time's hazy one. This time a fragment of an image emerged. It was as if someone had turned the focus dial on my mouth alone. I licked my lips just to be sure it was me. It was. I was getting clearer.

Chapter Fourteen

After I returned from Squeaky's five-dollar salvation cleanse, I realized I needed to devise a plan to take advantage of the Nightingale Loophole. But it had been a long day and I had a four o'clock date. Sort of.

The idea of a pseudo-date gave me a bellyache. I call it a pseudo-date because as I walked through the campus courtyard, I feared it would be a group date. Sprinkled among patches of broken sidewalk were hundreds of ripe, perky-breasted college girls. Their pony-tailed presence contrasted with the esoteric atmosphere of the English building, just as the distant neon lights of Circus Circus Casino contrasted with the intellectual mood of the century-old university campus.

The competition in Luke Marshall's classroom was intimidating. There were a dozen stunning female students, and one male, but I was sure he was gay. He had this cerebral look about him, and that, coupled with impeccable grooming and a metrosexual messenger bag, gave him away.

But the girls! Were college girls getting younger? Though I looked as nubile as most of them, I felt old. I walked past them to take my seat, and noticed them chomping bubblegum so intensely I could see most of their back molars in-between smacks. There wasn't one Jansport backpack in sight. Instead, they carried ultra-hip over-the-shoulder bags that screamed, "I'm hot. I'm casual. I just got laid."

One co-ed was writing with a bubblegum-pink gel pen, the kind I'd seen in the kids' section of Barnes & Noble. She mouthed a *secret* message to her girlfriend across the room. "He's . . . so . . . *hot.*"

She was pointing to Luke, whom I now considered my boyfriend. I shook my head at my new-found territoriality. Who was I kidding? I would be the worst girlfriend ever. I was emotionally unavailable, and my idea of a great date was one where I wasn't called away to kill someone. Anyway, he probably didn't even like me.

Just as I was pondering all this, and waiting for class to begin, the smallest silver cell phone in the universe bulleted toward me and hit me square in the nose. Then, as it spiraled to the floor, I noticed several lines of text on its LCD. Ponytail Girl in the back was using it as a means of communication. Okay, what happened to good old-fashioned note-passing?

"Oh, God!" the assailant screeched. "I'm so sorry. I was aiming for Carrie." She gestured to a girl in the front row who was laughing so hard I thought she might snot herself.

The way I saw it, I had two choices. One: Be cool, discreet, and hand the cell phone to the laugher, so she could read whatever message was important enough to maim her innocent classmate. Two: Read the message, assert my older, wiser, sophisticated self, and toss the phone back to her with a stern, "Watch it, girlie."

I glanced at the message.

> Really want to bone our teacher.
> Should tell him after class.
> What do U think?

Bone *my* boyfriend?! The game was on—survival of the sluttiest. She had the apple green bra and panties, but I had years of pent-up sexual energy. I decided to invent option three. I erased her message and replaced it with a new one.

When Ponytail Girl read my message—"Mine, Not Yours"—she received my other, more potent, more physical message. It began with a drip. Then single drips turned into a steady flow until, finally, her nose-faucet spewed cherry red blood down her front, soaking her clingy Abercrombie & Fitch sweater and ruining the bad writing in her teeny, tiny notebook. She cupped her nose with both hands and ran out of the room screaming.

Check.

The room got quiet—it was time to start class. Now everyone, even my new boyfriend, was looking at me. His hearing was so acute, as was his ability to assess his surroundings, that I almost forgot he was blind. He smiled and threw a friendly "shhh" my way.

Luke read us a brailed short story by Raymond Carver about a super observant waitress who serves a fat male customer. Luke's reading voice seduced everyone in the room, myself included, but I tried to pay attention. When he was finished, he asked us what we thought.

Ponytail Girl, who had recovered nicely, jumped in, making sure she got an "A" for the participation part of her grade. "I think the writer was trying to make a statement about the working class woman."

"Hmmm. I think that's trivializing the story a bit, Nan," Luke said without apology.

Nan—I hated her.

"Folks, I just got a memo," he said, picking up a blank piece of paper.

The gum-chomping stopped as a dozen girls tried to figure out if he needed it read to him. He crumpled up the paper and started laughing, as if he was half-kidding. "Do you know what the memo said? It said there would be no bullshitting this semester." He folded his hands. "Don't say things just because you think I want to hear them, because you'll be wasting everyone's time, including your own."

Nan sank in her seat. I wondered if she could take the heat, or if she'd drop this class for ballroom dancing or something less humiliating. Luke started up the discussion again, for fear he was "losing the crowd," as he put it, and everyone got more comfortable.

Then he called on me. He looked two inches to the left of my head, which was close enough for me, and flashed a ridiculous smile that said he was partly excited about keeping me on my toes, and partly sorry he was forcing me to talk. "Lucy, what did you like most about the story?"

Shit. Shit. Shit. I knew I should say something about the first-person narrator and how her point of view affected the story, but that's not what came out. What came out was, "Creamy fingers."

"Creamy fingers?" He walked over and sat on my desk, and I thought maybe he liked me. *Eat your heart out, Nan with the ponytail.*

"*Creamy fingers*," I said with confidence, "is just a kick-ass way to describe a man's chubby fingers."

He smiled again.

"Anyway," I said, "that's what I liked most."

"Honest response, Lucy." Then he walked his fingers up the binding of my book and closed it, indicating the end of class. But it was the way he closed it that made me blush. He shut it, then slowly moved it toward me, as if it was now my move.

Everybody left the classroom except for us. I was just about to ask him out for lunch when a male professor type, who evidently was a buddy, strolled in, looking at his watch. "So Lukey boy," the guy said, "did ya get lucky with the weird hottie, or am I fifty bucks richer?"

Luke's buddy didn't see me until he'd said too much. By their reactions, I knew they were talking about me. The buddy's eyes widened. He froze in place, walked backwards a few paces, then sighed and got out as fast as he could slither away. Luke closed his eyes and dropped his head.

"Lucy, it's not what you think."

Splotchy patches were already working up my neck toward my face—I had to leave, quick. "Great class. Thanks for inviting me."

He tried grabbing my hand, but I moved it out of his line of attack and shot out of the room. My nightmare unfolded as he and his candy cane clicked after me.

"Lucy, please stop. It was a stupid joke—that's all. I told him I was going to meet you at that Tupperware party and . . ."

I stopped in the middle of the hallway and told myself to think of something absurd to keep me from crying. *Monty Python's killer rabbit scene. Monty Python's killer rabbit scene. Monty Python's killer rabbit scene.* It didn't work. He placed his hand on my flushed face and froze when it made contact with a hot tear. I had to say something but couldn't.

"Stupid, stupid joke," he mumbled.

"I'm the stupid one," I said. "I gotta go."

"Don't go, Lucy. I didn't know you then. All I knew was that you were really hot, but a total recluse, and you liked Teddy Nightingale."

Well, no wonder then.

"But then at the coffee shop," he said, grabbing my hand, "I was pleasantly surprised. You're funny. And smart."

I looked deep into him, and I swear he saw me.

"And today, out of a roomful of women, you were the only one who mattered."

Someone needed to end this scene before it was ruined by a bad line. I pulled myself together. "Yeah, that's because I was the only one in there who doesn't have a curfew."

He looked relieved I hadn't slapped him yet, and he ran his hands through his hair. "Let me take you out to dinner. Please?"

There was no way to say yes without completely losing face.

"I'll think about it. I have your number." He was surprised. I turned around to make one last move. "So by *weird*"—I made quotation marks with my fingers—"your friend meant unique, original, and really special, right?"

He looked remarkably sorry.

Chapter Fifteen

The vast majority of Teddy Nightingale's songs are about love, and that fact justified stealing Luke's manuscript.

Yeah, I took it.

For love.

He had dropped the disk in the hallway as he was leaving the classroom in hot pursuit of me. After he finished defending himself, he scurried away, and the disk dropped out of his book bag. I copied its contents onto my hard drive and secretly returned the original disc to him that same night using a trick my supervisor taught me years ago. It was a long, complicated procedure, but I can tell you it involved an ancient spell and a thousand pounds of cayenne pepper.

Love has always been the strongest motivator. It made Orpheus gaze at and subsequently destroy Eurydice. It made Bonnie aid and abet Clyde. Actually, that's a bad example—she liked shooting people as much as he did. It made Whitney believe in Bobby's prerogatives. It made Hillary avoid castrating Bill—oops, another bad example.

Here's what matters: It made me want to be Luke's girlfriend at the most inopportune and absurd time in my life. I should've been putting all my energy into escaping my job, but I saw a possible romantic future in my hand—a floppy disk crammed with Luke's innermost thoughts.

I made a pot of coffee and sat down for a night of reading. When I inserted the disk, two file names popped up in the directory. The first was saved as "I want to shoot myself," and the other was titled, "No

Title." Curiosity prompted me to open the first one first. This is what I saw:

All work and no play makes Luke a dull boy.
All work and no play makes Luke a dull boy.
All work and no play makes Luke a dull boy.
All work and no play makes Luke a dull boy.
All work and no play makes Luke a dull boy.
All work and no play makes Luke a dull boy.
All work and no play makes Luke a dull boy.

It continued for forty-eight pages in a blurry but recognizable pattern. Was he a big fan of *The Shining*, or were the words just an insignificant way to let off steam?

At first, I thought it was some kind of joke—simple cut-and-paste word processing—but then I noticed the font changing every few pages, suggesting he had typed each phrase, each word, separately, because each new section was dated. The third section on page four, dated two weeks ago, featured a serious, bold font.

All work and no play makes Luke a dull boy.

Another page showed a happier, whimsical font.

All work and no play makes Luke a dull boy.

Page twelve, written two days later, must have been a bad day. Twelve lines looked like this.

All work and no play makes Luke a dull boy.

When I tired of the "Shoot Myself" file, I opened "No Title." Thirty-seven pages of his novel-in-the-making popped up. At the top of the first page, I saw what I assumed were working titles. Hmmm, can't make a decision? There were three: *Lying Still*, *Heart Land*, and *The Legend of the Corn Maiden*.

The first title was clever because of its duality: "Lying Still," as in "after all this time, I'm still not telling the truth," or "Lying Still," as in "I'm horizontal and motionless."

The second title was forgettable.

But the third title piqued my interest. I envisioned a voluptuous, nearly naked goddess whose flowing golden hair covered her heaving breasts. Her much too short corn husk skirt, which covered her from the waist down, made her the hottest corn maiden in the field.

Lying Still
Or
Heart Land
Or
The Legend of the Corn Maiden

by Luke Marshall

She had a Native American name, but she wasn't. I mean, she wasn't Native American.

She was blonde.

Her name was Tayanita. There was a story.

"My parents were into Indian shit," she said without looking at me as she slammed my drink down on the bar. When we made eye contact, she fluttered her cupped hand in front of her mouth, screeched an Indian chief noise that sounded more like Tarzan than Crazy Horse, and spoke in stereotypical, monosyllabic talk.

"Hey, 'One Who Ask Many Questions.' Five dollars or Tayanita scalp you."

I gave her a ten and waited for my change.

It never came.

After five drinks and twenty-five dollars in tips, she warmed up.

"My parents didn't name me until I was five days old. They were smoking the pipe when they wrote my name on the birth certificate. It was supposed to read Wakanda Hanson, but they accidentally wrote down Tayanita Hanson. Tayanita was right above Wakanda on the list of names they'd copied from The Most Popular Native American Names of 1969. *"*

"They're both good names," I assured her.

She folded her arms. "No, they aren't. They'd picked Wakanda because it means 'possessing magical power.' It's a strong Sioux name. My parents wanted me to be able to protect myself from evil forces, but they screwed up."

"Why? What does Tayanita mean?"

"Young beaver."

She recalled telling people the unfortunate and off-color meaning of her name.

"Seventh grade was the worst. Mrs. Brown, my social studies teacher, celebrated my unique name by making me a T-shirt for Cultural Awareness Day that said, 'Hi, my name is Tayanita. I am Young Beaver,' and forcing me to parade around the classroom in this headdress of plastic multicolored feathers she'd picked up at a truck stop in Utah."

"It could've been worse," I told her.

"How's that?"

"Tayanita could mean 'hard-working beaver.'"

I thought she'd laugh. Things had been going well. Instead, she picked up my glass and threw two ounces of perfectly good Wild Turkey in my face.

Chapter Sixteen

I stopped reading to replenish my coffee, but the cup overflowed as I thought how little I knew about the narrator, and how little I knew about Luke. I knew he could make me blush, and I knew he liked me in my dreams. After reading the first chapter of his story, I knew a few more things. He liked brief, terse sentences. And he knew what a beaver was.

I'd been scared I wouldn't like his work, but I did. I wondered if he liked lots of personal space the same way he liked lots of white space on the page, or if I should move in closer.

And what about this Tayanita? Who came first—me or her? All fiction shows glimmers of real life, so was Tayanita a girl he once knew? He obviously liked her.

I had no answers, so I made a to-do list. The last item was the most important but would also take the longest, so I put it last.

1. Write entry regarding Olivia Jakes.
2. Be more like Tayanita.
3. Quit my job.

I turned on my computer and after entering the usual—"Olivia Jakes. November 12, 10:45 a.m. Status: Expected"—I opened a blank file. Boss Man didn't want any details, just the facts, but the details were all I had, so I wrote them just for my benefit. As I wrote about Olivia Jake's demise, I tried to employ as much description as I could without overwriting.

After finishing my entry and drinking three glasses of wine to offset the effects of the coffee, I passed out. I was asleep for several hours when I heard something at my bedroom window. Too tired to move, I waited to hear it again. Something kept hitting the glass. When I walked over to see what it was, I saw someone standing in my front yard. I was just about ready to call 9-1-1 when he waved his cane and said my name.

It started out as a whisper and ended up as a full yell reminiscent of Marlon Brando in *A Streetcar Named Desire*.

"Luuuucy!"

The clock read 12:30 a.m. I wasn't in the mood for any unexpected drop-in clients.

"Lucy, it's Luke." He sounded drunk even through the window pane. "Luke Marshall. Your teacher." He whispered the last word, and when he did, I wondered what kind of NASA-inspired walking cane could lead a blind man, apparently inebriated, to my house in the middle of the night (although I supposed the time part didn't much matter). Did he pause for stoplights or, with an attitude, just *click-clack* his way through crosswalks?

I opened my window and, in the moonlight, saw him pick something up. Oh, no, Romeo. Not a guitar. I'd never before heard a drunk, blind man try to tune a guitar. It was painful. After twice dropping the instrument on the ground, he got it together and began to speak.

He stumbled a bit, but it was clearly a dedication. "This is for you, Lucy. A little birdie told me you'd like it."

By now, I was thoroughly awake and prepared to be entertained. I leaned out my bedroom window and tried not to be impressed.

"It's clear that . . ." and on the fourth word he started to strum the chords to a song I recognized. Not only was he cute, but he could hold a tune. ". . . the clouds come when you go away . . . what can I do to make you stay?"

He paused for a moment to get his fingering, and then started up again. "You're the light in my eyes," he sang. He stopped to burp. "You're my heart's grand prize."

Before long, I could tell he'd found his groove, because he tapped his foot and swayed back and forth. Just when I thought he was finished, he let out a passionate, "Here's the bridge, boys!" to his invisible band members, and changed his chords accordingly. "Since the beginning of time, we've all tried to find / a replacement for the power of love, / but I'm ready to unfurl, my heart's in a whirl, / and what I really need to tell you is . . . you're my girl." And with that, he dropped the guitar, took the key an octave higher, as Teddy always did, and got on his knees for the big finale.

I was nervous for him. I could tell it wasn't going as well as he'd liked, and he was banking everything on the *a cappella* ending. When Luke got to the chorus for the last time, he started clapping, the big-armed kind, and looked to me to play the participating audience role. Even I couldn't deny him in his delicate state, so I put my hands together out of good old-fashioned pity. In his head, I could tell he saw a luscious line of Rockettes kicking to the beat. I saw a man with his fly open asking for approval. At the end, he put his hands in the air, very proud of himself.

"How about that, Lucy Burns?" he said, then adding something about needing me back in his class. By the time I got downstairs, he was gone.

The next morning, I wasn't sure if I'd dreamt it or if he'd really been there, but I got my answer when I opened the door to bring in my newspaper. There was something sticking out from underneath my welcome mat. It was a receipt from the University of Nevada, Reno for $389.00. I was officially on the class list for ENGL 433, Creative Writing. He must have forged my signature on the add slip.

At the bottom of the paper, in messy handwriting, was this: "FYI: Homework assignment is attached. It's technically too late to drop, and your transcript can't take another 'W.' See you Thursday. LM."

Chapter Seventeen

I was still giddy from reading his note when I wrote out my to-do list for the day:

1. Call Maggie to plan our outing with Finn.
2. Deep-condition my hair.
3. Call Luke to let him know I don't hate him anymore.
4. Kill 54 serious, irredeemable sinners.

The first three were easy. The killing part would be more difficult. I'd never before damned that many people at once. Might it be smarter to do it in large chunks? And where would I find them? I decided to do a stream-of-consciousness free-writing exercise to brainstorm ideas. Below my to-do list, I wrote the word "evil" with lines jutting out from all sides, and wrote down the first things that came to mind. Child abusers. Rapists. Serial killers.

What I wrote down next ended up getting crossed out later, but it was my initial gut reaction: "Grocery store checkers wearing buttons that say, 'Paul from Sunnydale, California,' and who insist on commenting on everything I buy."

"Tampons and lighter fluid—sounds like you have a fun evening planned."

No comment, fuckhead!

Then I thought about those imbeciles who think out loud in movie theatres or bring their children to inappropriate films. Do I need to hear an old lady ask, "Is he dead?" every time someone gets shot? Or worse yet, little toddler Timmy asking, "Mommy, why's Hannibal eating brains?"

Once I got going, the list got easier. The newspaper helped. There were the greedy CEOs who spent their employees' pensions behind their backs. There were also the drug company CEOs who overcharged the elderly for their blood-pressure medicine—ordinary folks who merely hoped to have enough left over to buy cheap, crappy deli meat for lunch. Oh, and then there was the guy who sexually assaulted a young paraplegic woman in a wheelchair. If he had an address in the tri-state area, he was a goner. We could do without all of them.

Before I could execute a plan, I needed to know my due date, so I e-mailed Him. It's always awkward quitting a job but, for obvious reasons, this was trickier. What could I say? "I'm sorry, but I'm just not being challenged." That wasn't true. It was a hard job.

"I don't feel like there's room for advancement." That wasn't true, either. If I wanted to, I could become a supervisor.

And I couldn't say the job was completely unfulfilling, because on some level, it felt good discarding despicable people.

I decided to repeat what I'd said to my boss on quitting Baskin-Robbins during high school: "I feel I'm doing you a disservice by staying aboard." My boss was still unsure about my leaving, so I was forced to tell her how much peanut butter-and-chocolate ice cream I ate on the job without paying.

And that's what I told Him, that He'd be better off without me. He needed someone who would do a better job at meeting her quotas, someone who would stick to the facts, not inject emotion and an excessive number of adjectives into simple reports. There was no way I could tell Him I wished I'd never met Him, and how I hated Him with every ounce of my soul, assuming I still had one.

I hit "send" and felt sick, for fear of the expected backlash. To my surprise, I received a two-word response within minutes.

"December 25."

That couldn't be right. December 25th was only three weeks away. How was I supposed to complete all three tasks in that amount of time? Then the significance of the deadline hit me. Christmas. *Asshole!*

I had no choice, so I resumed my brainstorming. Serial killers? Too elusive. Hitler? Too dead. And then I remembered something I'd seen in the newspaper—an article about members of the Ku Klux Klan planning to protest the Gay Pride Parade taking place downtown.

Things were looking up, so I called Maggie.

"Hey, Lucy. Are we going to the zoo, or what?"

"Changed my mind, Mags. We're going downtown."

Chapter Eighteen

When I got to Maggie's house, she wasn't quite ready, so Finn and I shared some cookies and milk.

He seemed excited. "I looked up Teddy Nightingale's birthday . . . in *The Magic of Birthdays Book*. Wanna see?"

His index finger acted like a bookmark.

"Sure, let's read it together."

"Breaking free of your past will be your biggest challenge in life." Yeah, you and me both, Teddy. The last sentence was interesting: "There is an old adage that says, 'As ye give, so ye shall receive.'"

With a milk moustache in place, Finn asked what I knew he would. "What's that last sentence mean?"

"It means you have to give in order to get back."

A blank stare looked back at me.

I tried again. "It's like that good feeling you get when you give someone a gift. You're giving, therefore you're receiving."

He giggled. "We should just give out hundreds of presents to people, and then we'd get all sorts of stuff back."

I broke off a piece of the last cookie, and handed it to him. "It's not quite that easy, Finn. A real gift is one where you don't expect anything in return. To be pure, it has to come from the heart."

By the middle of that last observation, he'd lost interest, and I couldn't blame him. Finn jumped up to get his coat and whispered, "I forgot to tell you. My friend Justin—the one I thought I'd sent away—had chicken pox. He came back to school yesterday." I smiled and gave him a squeeze.

"Lucy," Maggie said, coming down the stairs, "did you hear about Olivia Jakes? Word is she left her husband a note saying she wasn't cut out to be married, and just took off. She's been gone since last week."

"Wow. Her husband's cute. Maybe I should call him."

"Lucy!"

"Just kidding. Hey, how's Karen Lowry doing?"

"Oh, I can't believe I forgot to tell you the good news. She's pregnant! Isn't that great?"

All was right on Sage Street.

Maggie grabbed her keys. "Okay, kiddo. What are we going to do downtown?"

After I told her, she looked at me with raised eyebrows. It was fun seeing her try to be politically correct.

"Lucy, God knows I don't believe in sheltering Finn, but . . ." she began to whisper. "He's only eight!"

I tried to rally. "Come on, Maggie. It's never too early to teach him about tolerance."

By the time we got downtown, the Gay Pride Parade was in full swing. Hundreds of gay men and women were busy celebrating their individuality. Some danced around with dramatic flare. Others walked around as if they were on a routine trip through the produce aisle. But none of them were the "I'm-a-little-bit-gay" types that kept their preferences under wraps. They were gay in a loud way. And they were cold. Nobody dared call them pansies—it took guts to go out in the northern Nevada winter wearing a tank top.

Although I had ulterior motives, it seemed like a good way to expose

Finn to other viewpoints. Some parade participants wore buttons professing "Hate Is Not a Family Value" and "Define Normal." We even heard a watered-down discussion about William Burroughs's line, "The only unnatural act is the one that cannot be performed."

But within minutes, we started seeing more colorful statements. It started with a hat featuring a ghost saying, "I see gay people," and by the time we saw the T-shirt asking, "Do you think my dick is too long for this skirt?" we decided to divert Finn's attention and head for the refreshments. We walked the yellow brick road over to the hot chocolate stand at the other end of the rainbow.

We had just ordered ours with whipped cream when I heard a woman with a microphone say, "You see that? These hate-mongers would rather see us dead than out here exercising our right to express ourselves."

She pointed at the clan, and I mean Klan, that had arrived in full uniform. I was stunned. I didn't think they existed outside of exploitative TV talk shows, and I never thought they'd be wearing hoods and full cloaks. I had counted on them coming, but when I saw them, I wondered if I could go through with it. Weren't they exercising the same rights as everyone else? Hate in any form is wrong, but I couldn't go around damning everyone who spoke up.

I sent Finn and Maggie over to a booth to buy a bumper sticker, and I snuck behind the sheet-wearing Klan members, only to find they weren't sheets at all—they were elaborate, strangely beautiful garments, customized for a perfect fit. What a job that must be, to sew for the Klan. What might alteration sessions sound like? "Could you take in the hood a little more? I want to look perfect for the 'White Is Right' rally."

In the commotion of shouting and marching, I spilled my hot chocolate all over a Klansman's freshly pressed cloak.

"Oh, my gosh, I'm so sorry," I said while wiping him down with a Kleenex.

When he answered, I realized he was a she. "Oh, don't worry about it. We dry-clean these things after every event."

So there we were, two women sharing a moment. I could've talked down to her because of what she represented, but after all, I too participated in my own brand of evil. It didn't seem possible for her voice to belong to someone who preached hate and intolerance, so I had to see for myself. I looked through the holes in her hood, and got her to hold still. This always came in handy when I was reeling in a potential client.

In a slow movement, I pulled up the cloth so I could see her face. In the bustling crowd, she stood motionless while I spoke into her ear, "Do you really believe these people don't have a right to live their lives how they want? Do you really think you have the authority to try to change them?" What she said was haunting.

"I believe God wants us to be pure. One white race. And only men and women together. Everything else is sacrilege."

"Do you think they deserve to die because they live like this?" I wondered if she and her bad hair were just one makeover away from rational thinking. A good color, cut, and manicure can change just about anyone. But then she spoke.

"'Whatever means necessary,' we say, to rid the world of these impurities."

"Just what I needed to know," I said as I pulled the hood back over her.

I pretended that my questions were a test, and that she'd passed. Then I handed her my card, telling her I could be a valuable resource for her cause.

"I'd like to meet the whole group. Why don't you bring everybody by my place tonight so I can show you what I can contribute. Bring as many as you want. Eight o'clock sound good?"

The way she looked at my name and address told me she would come. "That's great," she said. "But if anybody asks, I get credit for you—a new recruit over twenty-one gets me ten points. Only twelve points more and I hit my goal—a free pass to Silver Strike. Friday night is bowling night. You *are* over twenty-one, right?"

I nodded, realizing I'd been exposed to yet another pyramid scheme.

Maggie and Finn came back just as I finished, and saw nothing but me snapping my fingers to Diana Ross's "I'm Coming Out." On the way home, Finn asked why some people didn't like the parade marchers. Maggie's answer was that with freedom comes power, and some see that as a threat.

She was right. Freedom and power do go together, and I would need to use all my power to get free.

Chapter Nineteen

It's hard to know what to cook when the Ku Klux Klan comes over for appetizers. Something needed to be served, or they might get suspicious.

Another one of my motivations was more selfish—I needed the practice. It was time to develop some domestic skills, because it was possible I'd soon be re-entering the civilized world.

I ended up making little salmon and cream cheese tea sandwiches. Using the cookie cutter I got at the Pampered Chef party, I cut each one into the shape of a "K."

I'd intended to bake some goodies to bring to Luke when I saw him later, but I ran out of time, so I ordered a few small dessert trays from the Java House. I wanted him to think I made out-of-the-ordinary sweet treats, so I told them "no chocolate chip cookies, please," and made sure there were scones, tiramisu, baklava, and those little mini-muffins I pictured him fondling and inspecting with his hands.

My bigoted guests apparently took pride in being punctual—they arrived right on time. I was both relieved and disappointed when they walked in wearing just their street clothes. Floyd even brought a dish. He was a tall, lean man in his late thirties and, to my surprise, his blue eyes were warm and inviting. After I thanked him for his contribution, he said, "Oh, just a little family recipe," and handed me a rectangular metal pan filled with brown bananas held hostage in a pool of red Jell-O. I wondered if you could actually call foodstuff made of two ingredients a "recipe."

Floyd lifted into the air the duffle bag he'd brought with him. "Mind if I use your little boy's room? After this, I'm headed to my church-league basketball tourney." He winked, then said, "Contrary to popular belief, it *is* the white man's sport."

The other Ku Klux Klan members mingled a bit, pretending to be interested in the art up on my walls. Their closed mind-set made small talk unbearable, so I put on some music. I was thinking about my date with Luke, so my choice was simple. As soon as they heard it, they stopped talking and stared at me.

"Is this Air Supply?" said Hank, who had already eaten four Ks and three scoops of red Jell-O. "I love Air Supply."

That was it—these bastards were going to hell! "No," I said with mild indignation. "It's Teddy Nightingale."

They sat around my long dining room table for our suppertime feast. Some hummed to "You're the Light." Others ate bread and fish, and drank wine. Sipping turned to guzzling as they became unsettled, unsure why they felt agitated. This, of course, was my doing. The juxtaposition of Teddy's saccharin lyrics and the obvious tension growing in the room was unnerving for them. Some started squirming in their chairs; others looked at their watches.

At 9:10 p.m., the doorbell rescued me. I was eager to see my impressive dessert trays, but when I opened the door, I was horrified.

Goth-girl.

Of all the employees at the Java House, I had the misfortune of ordering on goth-girl's delivery day. As soon as she recognized me, she rolled her eyes and shook her head. "Where you want 'em?" she growled. Nobody else could possibly have understood what she said.

"Dog Speak," I whispered to Hank. "The latest rage."

I pointed to the coffee table, and decided I'd try to be civil to goth-girl—a second chance for a first impression. "Are you hungry? Would you like a cup of coffee?"

She snarled.

"Glass of wine? Prozac?"

"Forty-seven fifty," she barked.

So that was how she was going to be. I told her to relax while I looked for my checkbook, but arms folded, she followed me into the kitchen, where the Ku Klux Klan members were growing increasingly restless. Goth-girl raised her pierced eyebrows.

"Nice party. Somebody die?"

Wally and his buddy Muskrat rested their forearms, side by side, on my table and compared whose was whiter, then inquired about what I had to offer their organization. Goth-girl was on to them.

This time she spoke in English. "Fucking rednecks eating my fucking baklava. That's so fucking wrong!"

Things had escalated quicker than I thought. I didn't feel like trying to convert any of them, and I didn't want to discuss how screwed up they all were. I just wanted it done, so I did my thing. The eye contact. The mind control.

Goth-girl panicked, and ran over to my basement door, which I'd unlocked for the evening's festivities. Thinking it was an exit to the street, she flung it open. Pluto sniffed her and licked her combat boots, inviting her down. By the time she realized the door offered no outlet to the outside, but was an actual entrance to somewhere else, she was halfway down the stairs. And screaming.

Wait. Stop. Such a nice girl. What a shame!

When the others looked fully glazed over, Pluto corralled them into a tight formation. A part of me wished my victims had been in full dress uniform instead of sweatshirts and jeans. It just wasn't as dramatic as I'd pictured it.

It was over in two minutes—that's the good news. *The bad news?* There were only ten of them. Strike that—eleven. I still needed to find forty-three more bad souls. I'd need to pick up the pace. If I was going to complete all three tasks by the deadline, I needed to do some serious multi-tasking.

And the next task required me to answer this question: What kind of moron would want to take my job?

Before I had time to even get splotchy about it, I had my answer. She was right there in my living room. Before leaving, the Ku Klux Klan folks had forgotten to turn off the television, and from my couch, I had a perfect view of her. She was flitting about on some Hollywood entertainment show in a yellow Coco Chanel dress—strictly haute couture. I heard once that only two thousand people in the entire world can afford to indulge in true haute couture pieces, and being an heiress to the nth degree, she was one of them. Her parents owned a worldwide chain of resorts, and her life consisted of money, fashion, and . . . actually, that's it. Money and fashion.

It was as if she was auditioning for me but didn't know it. There were numerous shots of her mesmerizing everyone around her, moving to the head of the line at the hottest clubs, the ones that require massive amounts of money, fame, and silicone to be granted entry. There was endless footage of her executing double-cheek kisses, her lips in a constant state of pucker. She never missed a photo opportunity, and always looked the same: platinum blonde hair, charcoaled runway-model eyes, and a dress hiked up far enough to require pubic air-brushing.

The host asked her what it was like having everything, and she answered in that "I really want to be an actress" tone. "You all think I have it so easy, but let me tell you, my life can get really boring. I mean, it's the same clubs night after night, and all the fashion shows are starting to run together. I can't keep my Gucci straight from my Prada!"

She performed a sultry hair stroke, and the Ken-doll host tried to rub up against her boob.

She closed her eyes. "I'm just . . . I'm just really hungry for something new, something challenging. Everyone thinks I'm just some dumb blonde." She stared into the camera with her best on-the-verge-of-tears face. "But I'm not even a real blonde."

Then, pointing to herself, she let the cameras know she was about to announce something newsworthy, and armed with the power of an exclusive, they zoomed in to hear her talk about herself in the third person. "Venice is ready to give up the pampered life and do something good for the world."

So here was my girl—Venice Armada—the girl desperate enough to leave her past behind.

Did I have the perfect job for her!

Chapter Twenty

The next day, I took a break from my tasks. I should've hit the streets looking for more clients, but it was Thursday and that meant I had a legitimate reason to see Luke. He looked pleased when I showed up for class, especially after I discreetly put a plateful of baked goodies under his desk, but Nan (formerly known as Ponytail Girl) was unenthused, so I sat down beside her to cause maximum irritation.

We both looked at the sentence written on the board: "Plot is a verb." I wondered if Nan knew what a verb was. I did, and I was relieved to see it on the board, because it meant I'd done my homework assignment right. We were supposed to write a "short piece of fiction." That's it—no other guidelines.

The first piece I wrote (then threw away) was dark, subtle, and boring—my attempt at being literary. There were several long passages, rich with metaphor and description, about a woman exploring her tendency to be un-nurturing. It was more of a character piece, but the character wasn't interesting, because she didn't do anything. The story was just a series of flashbacks in which she recalled all the things in her life she'd killed: ferns, hermit crabs, canaries.

The second piece I wrote was about a woman who, after losing her husband—and by "losing," I mean he died—embarks on a quest to find Bigfoot. She doesn't care what he is called—Sasquatch, Yeti, Skunk Ape, Yowie, or Forest Man—she just wants to find him.

The story begins with her and her two children in the middle of a forest in the Pacific Northwest, looking for something everyone said didn't exist—something she is convinced would heal the gaping hole in her family. Through flashbacks, I reveal that her husband used to dress up as Bigfoot on family camping trips to entertain and subsequently scare the bejeezus out of the kids, but after their father's death, the kids wonder where the beast is, or if he still exists.

And if he ever existed at all.

My story was an odyssey fueled by faith, but as I saw everyone else's papers, just five or six pages in length, I knew mine had guzzled too much fuel. As class began, Luke asked us to put our stories in a pile on his desk. Too embarrassed to bring mine up, I pawned it off on Nan, who rolled her eyes but took it up for me.

By the sentence on the board, I knew that choosing my plot-driven story was a good choice, although my not-so-short short story might have exceeded the instructor's limited patience. I had tried to imitate Luke's terse writing style, but I wasn't concise. I was verbose. Coming in at forty-seven pages, my story fell to his desk with an alarming thud, and as it dropped, I realized it would take his assistant three days to Braille it for him.

Plot ran out of every orifice in my body, and plot, for me, was indeed a verb—I wanted to dash out of the room, tear down the hallway, and run all the way home. Maybe I could play it all as a joke. I wondered if he'd believe I spent that much time writing a novella just to get a good laugh.

Class that day was devoted to the notion of plot, and the bad rap it got in the world of character-driven fiction. The discussion started with Luke putting major events from the Cinderella story on a traditional plot line. When he got to the part where the prince finds her, I swore I heard a chorus of "awww's" coming from the post-pubescent, gumchomping sluts pretending to be college students. They all sat up a little straighter when he said "denouement."

The girl next to Nan whispered loudly enough for me to hear, "God, I bet he speaks, like, ten different languages."

I was in a roomful of Cinderellas who traveled light in every sense of the word—tiny tote bags, tiny asses, and even cute, tiny homework papers. And me, I was the heavy step-sister, lugging around twenty years of excess baggage and a gigantic story about an erect bipedal monkey who represented hope.

As class continued, I found myself obsessing about my mound of a story sitting on his desk. Everyone seemed to be glancing at it and giggling. Before I knew it, Luke was ending class with a clarification on an age-old tenet for writers.

"The universal advice to writers is to 'write what you know,' but let's face it, none of us is all that interesting."

I imagined what Nan and her cohorts might have written about—a character, like totally fictitious, who got severely burned in a tanning bed, and had to spend the semester in a turtleneck.

Luke finished with one final bit of truth.

"Stories need to be more than mere character sketches. They must document what a character does. The narrative has to move forward," he said, his sightless green eyes darting back and forth in a think pattern, "because life has to move forward."

He projected those words toward me, as if he knew I needed help moving my own life forward.

Everyone left, and it was just us.

"Well, here we are again, Professor Marshall." I gave him my coyest schoolgirl look, even though he couldn't see it. "Or am I supposed to call you Dr. Marshall?"

"Luke. Luke is fine." His smile made me want to touch my hair, so I did.

"You do a mean Nightingale, Luke," I said in teasing sarcasm.

"Right. I was hoping you might have blocked that out, as one would a traumatic event."

Moving closer to him, I wondered if his heightened sense of hearing would detect my thumping heart and give me away. "Consider it done.

Blocking out traumatic events is my specialty."

"Interesting." On a scale from one to ten, ten being the naughtiest, I would've given his smile right then an eight. He folded his hands and leaned back on his big desk. "You'll have to wait to find out *my* specialty."

The energy needed to formulate a witty comeback was spent sorting out the butterflies in my stomach, so without thinking, I took his hand in mine. By now I was sure my pounding chest rivaled Poe's "Tell-Tale Heart," so I was relieved when he rescued me.

"How about you pick me up at seven, and we'll celebrate Teddy Nightingale, traumatic events, and that homework you just turned in?"

Big mouth Nan must have made a snide comment about the "thud" being *my* assignment.

I smiled extra hard so he could feel it. "Okay."

When I got home, I resumed reading Luke's story. I wanted to learn more about him before our date. By page twelve, I'd discovered who the narrator was.

Jack—a writer who no longer wanted to write.

He'd graduated with an English degree, spent some time in the prestigious Writer's Workshop, but then, upon graduation, became uninspired. To make rent, he took a job editing minor publications for the Iowa Corn Growers Association, and became proficient at fitting obscene amounts of information about corn-related issues into glossy, four-color, tri-fold brochures.

The copy Jack had to edit was usually a mess. Someone *always* misspelled "ethanol." On top of the hideous grammatical errors, there was the sheer monotony of it all. Who makes the better combine, John

Deere or International? Which type of feed produces a better yield?

To keep from daydreaming, he often made up corn-related jokes that started with "How many farmers does it take to. . ." or "Your mama eats so many bushels of corn that . . ."

I wondered if Luke even liked corn.

Hoping to find out more about Luke via Jack, I continued with Chapter Three of *The Legend of the Corn Maiden*.

One week after our angry encounter, I went to the Deadhead again to see Tayanita. I'd thought about her every day for a week. I imagined her behind the bar, comfortable and naked, calling me an asshole. She'd become my muse.

The muse was unimpressed with my return. "Whiskey again?"

I wanted to say something smart like, "Wakanda, O magical one, use your powers to buy the house a round," but I didn't want her to know I remembered her other name—the one her parents were too stoned to give her. It would make me appear desperate. The stalker vibe is never sexy.

"Come here often?" I asked.

She heard me but walked to the end of the bar. Every man there had a crush on Tay. They called her the Corn Maiden because of her favorite Sioux legend. She was 5'10," but her feminine curves made her seem more voluptuous than tall. And her au naturel, no-makeup face, which was sprinkled with light freckles, made her wavy blonde hair seem more bohemian than cheerleader.

She told a mean yarn.

They sat on the edge of their barstools as if she was a newscaster delivering the news of certain Armageddon. Her delivery and timing were deadpan, never animated; she didn't have to be. She was "the Corn Maiden."

I needed to leave soon for our big date, so I read the rest of chapter three, devouring it as one would digest *Cliff's Notes* before an exam.

Important Vocabulary: *Maiden*: unmarried girl or woman. *Trickster*: one who makes up for weakness with cunning. *Victor*: one who defeats an adversary.

Central Themes: Duality. Truth. Transformation. Justice.

Plot Summary: Tayanita, both a joker and a truth-teller, a creator and a destroyer, tells stories to a bar full of lost souls. Each story stars "the Trickster," infamous for bringing chaos to the natural order of things.

"A coyote, right? The Trickster is always a coyote," said a voice from the last barstool.

Tayanita mixed one last gin and tonic. "Not always," she said.

Chapter Twenty-One

A pang of nausea raced through my stomach just as I began primping for my date with Luke. It was an unfriendly reminder to keep Luke in the "Friend Zone," at least for now. If I wanted to stay smitten with him, I'd have to keep my hormones under control.

All this sex business affected my clothing choice, because I didn't want my date outfit to send the wrong message. For a blind man, he was very visual. At the coffee house, he wanted to know every detail of my clothing, right down to the rip in the left leg of my Levi's.

Hmmm. What would Tayanita wear? Nope, can't do earthy-chic. I ended up choosing a heather gray, pinstriped pencil skirt, extra form-fitting, and a crisp, white blouse exposing a healthy supply of cleavage.

When I picked him up, he demonstrated his sixth sense. Or was it just his fifth, because he was missing one? He put one hand on the warm hood of my still-running car, closed his eyes, then raised his other hand in the air as if he was going to sneeze, and said, "Shhh."

Luke and his candy cane were propped against my car, conducting what looked to be an auto-exorcism. His hand stroked one of my headlights, and I was jealous. Then, using his fingertips as eyes, he examined the car's silhouette. At the height of every curve, he raised one eyebrow.

After feeling his way over the entire outline, the two side windows, the bumper, and the door handles, he stopped. He looked proud of himself. "General Motors. 350. 1967." Pause. "No. 1968." The hood became a makeshift pillow when he put his head down on it. Calmly, he announced, "It's a Camaro."

Luke listened carefully to the ticking motor, and when it hiccupped every few seconds, he answered with a head nod. After their secret conversation was over, he gave my car a friendly pat, and said, "Cool."

"Okay, smarty," I said, "what color is it?" As soon I said it, I regretted how mean I sounded.

"Red. Not a cherry red. More like a . . . burgundy."

I was relieved he couldn't see my surprise. "How did you . . ?"

He brushed it off as no big deal. We got in the car, and all he wanted to talk about was what I was wearing. By the time I finished describing my shoes, we'd arrived at our destination.

A La Carte-Blanche was Luke's favorite restaurant, and I knew why immediately upon arrival. As its name implied, the notion of choice was paramount. The décor was, in fact, a clean slate—white walls, white tablecloths, white dishes.

It was so blank it made me want to take a black marker and scribble random thoughts on every flat surface. I imagined penning "sea turtle" on the white door, "lemon meringue" on the white-tiled floor, and "serendipity" on the milky-countered bar. The décor celebrated the beauty of all things minimal, and in a city of excess, it was downright refreshing. None of this could be seen by Luke. But he felt it.

Unlike the casino restaurants, this one was also devoid of flashing lights or neon. The candlelit seating area took on a golden hue, which flickered just enough to cast mini-shadows. As we sat down, the lights above us dimmed, and our waiter lit a votive at our table.

Luke took a deep breath. "It's nice here, isn't it?"

When I handed him a menu, he laughed and gave it back to me. "Everything's *a la carte*. You get to choose your own combinations." He walked his fingers over to my menu, and with the strangest luck, pointed right at the potato section. "So, Lucy Burns, you can have potatoes—French fries *and* garlic mashed—if you so desire."

"You like that, don't you?" I said.

His smile started slow, then ended in a big, peaceful grin. "I like options, if that's what you mean. And I like filling in the blanks. I've had lots of practice."

His life was one long, extended series of filling in the blanks the rest of us took for granted, like whether or not a sunset looked peachy-pink and hopeful, or the way a woman's eyes looked when she was smitten.

I could tell he wanted to change the subject. "Speaking of having lots of practice, I haven't read your story yet, but wow, it's long. Did you write it, or did you just print out fifty pages from *Encarta*?"

He took a drink of his wine and waited for me to laugh at his joke, but all he heard was the ice clinking in my water glass.

"That didn't come out right. I'm sure it's fantastic. I can't wait to read it. Hey, it's more than I'm writing right now."

I imagined what Tayanita would say to Jack, and then said something nicer. "Oh, please. I'm sure you've got the Great American Novel saved on your computer, waiting to be revised and printed."

He took another drink. "No, I'm stuck. All I have are great first lines."

At first, I thought his self-deprecation was aimed at making me feel better, but he continued.

"One line, and then it all goes to shit. Every time I teach a class, I feel like a fraud. I haven't written a decent piece of fiction for five years. Maybe I should just stick to writing academic articles."

I wanted to comfort him, but I didn't want to appear servile. "Oh, come on, there's got to be a good story in one of those first lines. Hit me."

He was nervous. For once, I felt in control.

"Okay, here's one." He cleared his throat. "Anne couldn't decide if she should kill herself or eat a tuna fish sandwich."

I let two waiters pass by before I answered, just to make him wonder what I was thinking. "Try another one."

His mouth dropped. "Oh my God. You're harsh. Was it that bad?"

But before I could answer, he revealed another line. "Okay, here's a good one." He straightened his napkin. "Deer are committing suicide all over town."

He was so cute, it was ridiculous. Trying to seem disinterested made my head throb.

Grinning, he said, "It's a story about male deer crashing through glass windows when they see their own reflection during rutting season."

I thought of men, in the heat of competition, trying to court women at bars, then smiled.

"You twirl your hair when you don't know what to say," he commented.

I hadn't realized that until he pointed it out.

I stopped. How did he know that? "I was just going to say, Mr. Impatient, that I like both sentences very much, but aren't you a bit obsessed with death? Or is it that you find deer and tuna sandwiches to be particularly ominous topics?"

"That's enough about me." A long pause. "Who is Lucy Burns?"

All of a sudden, my appetite disappeared. Even a la carte shrimp became inedible. Talking about me would be a disaster, but I had to say something. And then it just flew out of my mouth.

"I'm allergic to nuts." I had no idea why I said it. I loved nuts.

"That's not *you*. That's a medical condition. Come on, don't be a chicken. I thought you were tough, Lucy Burns."

It felt as if we were playing truth or dare at a slumber party. Truth was the hardest part of that game. No matter how old I was, I hated being called chicken. It was such a ten-year-old thing to say, but it worked.

"Okay, okay." I was stalling—I still had nothing. I then started stuffing shrimp in my mouth, one after another, until I got up the nerve to speak, and when I did, he couldn't understand me.

"Well, I do what I can." I wiped my mouth off and began to stumble. "I'm in the middle of . . . I'm trying, really trying, to pull my life together, Luke. It's a certifiable mess." And then pure, honest silence. No follow-up joke, no looking around the room to change the subject. I remained quiet to give him an out. "So," I added finally, "if you're looking for someone uncomplicated, I'm not your girl."

"I see." He folded his arms.

I knew things didn't look good when he asked for the check. It was the shortest dinner date ever. Even the waiter was surprised we were leaving so soon. Why was I so damn truthful? I should've lied.

"So, 'Complicated Lucy,' would you like to see where a starving writer hangs his hat?"

It felt good to be surprised.

"Sure."

Chapter Twenty-Two

When we walked inside his house, a charming 1930s bungalow, I saw a familiar sight—de Chirico's *Mystery and Melancholy of a Street*. I walked over to it.

"I have this one, too," I said.

From the kitchen, he shouted, "Really? I hear it's really cool," and then delivered my glass of chardonnay. He moved around his house without hesitation, as if he had a blueprint in his mind. He motioned for me to sit down on the couch, and a sighted man couldn't have placed himself more perfectly—he sat close enough to touch my leg with his hand, but not in a creepy, you're-crowding-me sort of way.

He had a confidence about him, and as I studied his smooth movements and periodic smirks, it occurred to me I'd been had. "That whole thing with my car," I said. I shook my head. "I'm such a fucking idiot."

"No. I'm just really persuasive." He smiled and put his hand on my knee.

"How did you find out?"

"That bitchy girl at the coffee house described your car when you went to the bathroom—you were parked in a handicap spot."

"Cheers," I said, feeling a tad guilty about goth-girl.

When our glasses met, we both smiled as if we were at a high school dance. He moved closer, and although I wanted him to kiss me, I pulled away.

"Lucy, I didn't ask you here to sleep with you, in case you were wondering."

I hid behind my glass. "Sorry, I'm not used to dating."

"Don't get me wrong. I'd love to—" He'd fallen into a hole he couldn't scratch his way out of. "I'd love to be that person for you but, believe it or not, I'm a gentleman."

"Perhaps the only one left in Reno," I said.

"Does that make you nervous—the thought of us getting physical? These awkward silences are killing you, aren't they?"

I denied it all. "It's not you . . ."

He smiled and rocked his head back and forth. "Oh, no. Let me guess, it's not *me*, it's *you*."

The mood turned dismal despite the wine consumption.

"But it *is* me."

Under his breath, he said, "I should've known."

Now I felt bad. I leaned into him and turned his face to mine. "Known what? What should you have known?"

Still sitting cross-legged, he ran his hands through his hair, trying to look casual. "Look, Lucy, it's no big deal. I should've known this was going to happen. Your not being attracted to me. I mean . . . you can have anybody you want." His ego had arrived, and his body language grew defensive. He uncrossed his legs, folded his arms, and turned his head away from me.

"Don't be mad, but that was my only reservation about you—how good-looking you are. My buddy said it's unnatural." He again ran his hands through his hair and sighed. "God, this went to a place I didn't want to go. I'm totally out of line. Just forget everything I said."

I started to chuckle. "No, this is great. So, you're telling me that if I were short, flat-chested, and fat, you would keep dating me?"

"How *much* fatter?" he asked.

I hit him in the arm. He never saw it coming.

"Kidding!"

At that moment, the urge to kiss him felt like the urge to eat, to breathe, to devour that last chip in the Dorito bag. I wasn't sure if I could resist. After all, nobody had prohibited me from kissing. Besides, at that moment, if my choices were to be liberated from my oppressive job, or to kiss Luke, I would've made it the longest kiss ever. But we didn't. Instead, I spotted a high school yearbook on his bookshelf and picked it up.

"Class of 1992. Let's find Luke Marshall. Or were you Lucas then?"

He rolled his eyes, preparing to be humiliated.

On page forty-nine, I found the man of my dreams, only he had a mullet-like haircut. Touching his head, I said, "Business in the front, party in the back."

"Stop." By now he was hiding behind his hands.

I kept going. "Wisconsin waterfall."

He grabbed the book, but as it left my hands, the pages flipped and I saw someone I recognized toward the front.

"Let me see that again."

"I'm not wearing parachute pants, if that's what you're checking."

There she was. "Is that who I think it is?"

"Yeah, yeah," he sighed. "We went to high school together. A *friend*. We had chemistry together—the class, I mean. My father did business with her father."

"Let me guess, at the country club?"

"This is where I tell you I'm from Beverly Hills and you leave thinking I'm a trust fund baby squandering his life and his inheritance."

"Are you?"

"I went to college in Iowa and became a teacher out here to get away from the shallow L.A. scene. That's it. End of story."

So I'd found Luke's tender spot, and I'd discovered he knew someone I desperately needed to meet.

On my way out, he asked when he could see me again.

I tried to sound confident. "Tomorrow night," I said.

As I got ready for bed, I wondered what life with Luke would be like. With an imaginary pen, I imagined writing "Lucy Marshall" in various cursive styles, and that night, he came to me, in a dream.

Luke, Tayanita, and Teddy were all there. At first, I couldn't see them—I only saw a giant wall of white canvas. But as often happens in my dreams, my subconscious painted in the details with slow brush strokes. Black first. Several swipes later, Teddy's grand piano emerged. Then yellow. Tayanita's corn-maiden hair cascaded down the white backdrop in shiny, golden swirls.

As soon as they were both fully formed, they took a breath and sang in unison. Teddy's melody and Tay's harmony took flight—eventually, hundreds of black, curvy winged notes morphed into little black "L"s and lined up to create a mosaic-style Luke.

And in a complex configuration made up of every color "L" imaginable, Luke appeared. He sat at his desk writing the same word over and over. I couldn't make it out right away, but as the string of identical words spilled into the white space and wormed its way over to Teddy and Tayanita, the word became clear.

"Choice."

Chapter Twenty-Three

The phone woke me the next morning. It was my supervisor using her "who do you think you are?" voice. "It's come to my attention, Lucy, that you want to leave us. How tragic. Tell me how you think you'll pull this off."

I told her I knew about the loophole.

"Interesting. Great. Super," she said as if talking to a kindergarten class. "I thought you *had* a life—a quite lavish life, in fact. You do realize that by returning to 'normal,' as you put it, you'll be just that—normal. Normal means being a powerless size fourteen who wears shoes from Payless, drives a Dodge Stratus, and works overtime just to afford a crappy annual vacation to Jamaica, only to find when she gets there, she's too fat to go to the beach, and settles for getting her hair braided by a local stoner!"

"I'm sorry you feel so strongly about it, but my mind's made up. I've corresponded with Him. I need to do this."

"Fine. Spin your privileged little wheels all you want, but you still have work to do." Her disgust seeped through the receiver, and I knew she was rolling her eyes like a teenage girl. "This week's house call is very routine—Peter Lindeman."

A house call was when I had to venture into the outside world and meet a client on his own turf. These types didn't leave their homes enough to drop in at my residence, meaning I had to go to them.

"How am I supposed to explain being at his house?" I asked.

"You're the Facilitator, Lucy. Facilitate."

I'd seen Mr. Lindeman's type on *60 Minutes* a couple months earlier. They preyed on the elderly by selling them bogus life insurance policies. The stories were heartbreaking. The CBS reporter choked up when an eighty-year-old woman explained how she'd lost her entire savings to a guy like Peter Lindeman. All Bessie Danielson wanted was to leave her hard-earned money to her grandchildren, but instead she gave it to a criminal who used some of the money to buy his girlfriend Chrissy some new, perky double-Ds.

Though I felt bad for the victims of Peter Lindeman and his ilk, I wasn't all that motivated to get rid of him, primarily because he wouldn't count as one of the forty-three people I still had to banish. I needed to think through my plan for Peter, but when I began writing his entry, I opened my personal journal instead.

Page after page, I ranted about my predicament. Then I heard Teddy's voice: "The real portal—the mother of all portals—has an unusually powerful lure."

That was it! Screw this one-at-a-time bullshit. I needed to think big, though I immediately worried if damning in bulk would result in a discounted number.

In any event, my most powerful resource was only five miles away.

When I pulled up outside Peter Lindeman's house, I double-checked the address. I always did when making a house call—for obvious reasons. It turned out to be the right place—a modest brownstone on the smart side of downtown.

I touched the metal front door with the palm of my hand, immediately feeling guilt and regret. This was often how it worked. Emotions, some too painful to bear, settled in my *clients'* surroundings—sometimes in their furniture, sometimes in their vehicles. In this case, the structure of Peter's home had absorbed his sins. The denser the substance, the easier it was to sense it, like feeling vibrations in an aluminum bat on a chilly spring day.

I knocked on the door, and when he answered, I greeted him with a flirty hair toss.

"I'm so sorry to bother you. My car ran out of gas, and this is the first house I came to with lights on." As I spoke, I looked deep into his eyes. It wasn't hard convincing him to let me in.

It's difficult to explain my ability to carry out mind control—by then, it had become second nature to me. But the best way to describe how it feels is to compare it to shivering. That's how it starts. I'd force a fake-shiver, which would start in my arms. Then the tingling would shoot through my body, doubling, then tripling, until it would explode into a firestorm of electricity in my belly. Once it reached the desired strength, I'd concentrate it into an invisible ball, and wherever I directed it, it traveled. Whoever it came in contact with did whatever I wanted.

"Here." He invited me in. "You must be freezing."

His house was immaculate. The hardwood floors were buffed to a glossy sheen, and the fluffed-up throw pillows on his designer sofas were strategically placed. His kitchen, a stainless steel dream, was a cityscape of high-performance industrial appliances. It was the kind of kitchen that housewives have in mind when they purchase lottery tickets.

As I thought about all the old people who'd lost everything because of his shenanigans, his furnishings began to take on a sinister look to me.

He offered me some hot tea, and said he might have some spare gas for me in a container in the garage.

While the water boiled, we talked about him. "You know," he said, and right then he started sounding like a used car salesman, "if you had Triple-A, you could just call for some gas or a free tow. Insurance is so important." He used a patronizing voice. "I sell insurance. It makes people feel good, feel safe. How are you on life insurance?"

I couldn't believe it. He was actually trying to sell me life insurance. *Me!* Because I didn't want to be there all night, I began to scour his home for anything that might help me with my plan. And there I spotted it—his little black book.

I "T-squared him." That's the abbreviation for a trick my supervisor calls the "Temporary Trance," the kind I used when I needed only a few minutes to finish a task. Lindeman sat, blank-faced, in his leather wing-back reading chair while I perused his address book.

I was right. Unlike most men, Peter Lindeman didn't have a book full of ex-girlfriends. He was, purely and simply, a greedy, amoral entrepreneur. His book had the e-mail addresses of all his sales people. I knew these underlings were local, because my supervisor said the only time Peter left his house was to meet one of them, but mostly he corresponded with them via e-mail to provide them their targets.

When I had the information I needed, I woke him with a sharp snap of my fingers. Still under my power, he agreed to come back to my house, where he promised to quickly produce the paperwork necessary for a life insurance purchase.

As soon as we got there, Peter Lindeman surprised me. Though I had a strong hold on him, I must have lost concentration when I heard Pluto begin to bark. Somewhere between the living room and the kitchen, Peter became defiant.

"I've got to go," he said, blinking several times. "I don't think I want to sell you insurance anymore." He looked at Pluto, who was growling and foaming at the mouth, and started to run toward my front door. He froze when Pluto magically appeared and blocked his escape route. Peter scanned the room for possible weapons, but ended up staring at the girl in the de Chirico painting.

Noticing the tall shadow looming around the corner, he must have felt a kinship with her—a solidarity with another unsuspecting victim. We walked away from the painting, leaving the girl in a frozen state of vulnerability, and when I walked to the basement door, Pluto finished the job.

I went back to his house, and using his little black book as a directory, e-mailed all twenty-one of his underlings, pretending I was Peter. I told them to meet me the following night at Vesuvius Village, at the entrance to the Bestia roller coaster.

I knew they'd think it odd, but it was how we were handing out Christmas bonuses this year, I wrote. I hoped the lure would be strong enough that, though they might feel suspicious when they got there, they would feel defenseless and stay.

The next morning, Maggie asked me to drive Finn to school. He'd missed the bus, and David had driven the truck to the hardware store. Finn reached his small hand deep into his canvas book bag. It had "Finn" imprinted in orange letters at the top. "Wanna see my show-and-tell?"

"It'd be the highlight of my morning, Finnster."

He pulled out his latest school project, a God's Eye. Two crossed twigs provided a framework for four sections of tightly woven purple, yellow, and green yarn, which created a rainbow-like spider web's effect.

In third grade, I'd written a report on God's Eyes. "Finn, did you know that variations of these exist in almost every culture and religion?" I thought of Tayanita and the Corn Maiden.

"My library book said it's a window that God can look through to talk to people who need help."

I patted his knee. "Nice job, hon." When I stopped at a red light, he placed it between us on the red leather seat hump and looked at me.

"Do you want to talk to it?"

Did he think I needed to? "Sure. Maybe next time I come over to babysit."

Undeterred, he slowly pushed it toward me with his eight-year-old index finger. "We still have time before we get to school." He looked at it, then me, as if he was waiting for something to happen.

I needed coffee. "How about we go to McDonald's and get some hotcakes?"

"Sure."

It was a diversion and he knew it. Just before we got to school, he put the God's Eye in his bag and exited the car. He got halfway to the school doors, then ran back and knocked on the passenger's window. I leaned over and unrolled it.

"Forget something, babe?"

He flashed a knowing look. "I'll talk to it for you, if you want."

I smiled at him. "Finn, tell the class it's an *ojo de dios*."

He repeated *ojo de dios* as best he could. "See you tomorrow?"

"See you tomorrow, Finn."

A big day lay ahead of me, so when I got home, I immediately prepared my to-do list:

1. Find out when and where my date with Luke is.
2. Make a batch of hallucinogenic brownies for my late-night

roller coaster seductees.

3. Get a hold of Luke's latest chapters of *Corn Maiden*.
4. Do my homework.

I painted my toenails blood red while talking into the speaker phone. "Dr. Marshall? This is Lucy Burns. I'm calling to complain about this week's homework."

He laughed. "Nobody likes a whiner, Miss Burns."

"Write something with a 'supernatural element'? To me, that doesn't seem very literary."

He played along, using his best teacher voice. "It's just an exercise, Miss Burns—a crutch, if you will . . . a place to start when looking at that daunting blank page."

"I heard once that a blank page is God's way of showing you how hard it is to be God."

"Interesting, Miss Burns. Perhaps we should discuss this in person. Meet me for a drink at Duffy's. Eight o'clock?"

"Doesn't that violate the teacher-student relationship?"

I could tell he was smiling. "*Violate.* Your word, not mine." He sounded like Luke again. "You know Duffy's? By the Pompeii Casino?"

"Eight o'clock it is."

After hanging up with Luke, I made two dozen brownies, adding a little something to help relax the boys in case the portal wasn't as strong as Teddy said it was. If all twenty-one Lindeman cohorts actually showed up, I'd still have twenty-two more people to banish to meet my quota of fifty-four.

My deadline was only six days away, and none of my tasks had been completed yet. Where could I find another twenty-two horrible human beings? I turned on the morning news for ideas, but was disappointed when every news story featured some act of goodness, selflessness, or heroism.

The whole world, it seemed, was suddenly full of decent people.

It was awful. Firemen rescued cats, and grade school kids became pen pals with recovering crack-addicts. Five local housewives raised enough money in a bake sale to send thirty attention-deficit-disordered sixth-graders to Europe. It was one random act of kindness after another.

What the hell happened to all the bad people? I didn't live on a farm—this was Reno, for God's sake! There had to be some kind of terrible deed—I'd even take an act of animal cruelty—committed during the past twenty-four hours. I was so desperate, I thought I might have to send to Hell some guy who'd bounced a couple of checks.

But then I had a revelation. I, too, could be a philanthropist. I'd call it Alternative Placement Rehabilitation.

I whipped out my to-do list and added this item:

5. Win over some prison inmates.

Chapter Twenty-Four

As I drove to Carson City, Nevada, home of the Nevada State Penitentiary, I was thinking of Teddy Nightingale's tune "Lock Me Up." The song is about a guy doing prison time, and I wondered which would be worse—knowing I was never leaving prison, or knowing I was never leaving Carson City, Nevada.

As in Reno, there were several casinos in Carson City, except they were smaller, smokier, and more geriatric-friendly.

I stopped at a crosswalk to let two men with walkers scoot across the street toward the Mother Lode, the biggest of the little casinos. But halfway across, right in front of my car, the duo came to a halt. Each put a wrinkled hand up to his ear to indicate his inability to hear the other. The cigarettes dangling from their mouths didn't help the matter, because as soon as one puckered mouth would mumble something, the other puckered mouth would mumble, "Huh?"

When I honked to get their attention, one of them hollered an obscenity, the cigarette dropping from his mouth. As he bent over to get it, he and his walker collapsed in slow motion. An unmoving heap of skin, bones, and metal lay before me on the concrete. I jumped out and helped him up, while both geezers called me various sexist epithets.

After getting the guys to the curb, I couldn't help but feel dissatisfied with my good deed. Was this the life they'd dreamt about? Didn't they have grandkids playing baseball somewhere, or had they turned down family life in exchange for nickel slots and Friday night six-pack dinners? I envisioned them spending their winnings on better, more high-tech walkers and extra trips to the prime rib buffet.

I arrived at the prison a bit behind schedule. A few feet inside the gates, three straight-faced prison guards stood with folded arms. I unbuttoned my stretch velvet pea coat just enough for them to see what I wanted. I felt ridiculous. Here I was, at a maximum security prison, wearing a clingy black dress and heels. But I needed to be one hundred percent vamp to pull this off.

I showed them my fake identification, and told them I had an appointment with the chief warden. They frisked me—a bit too long, I might add—then sent me through to the next guard station.

My plan was to recruit as many "clients" as I could stir up, but it was harder than I thought. While I walked through Cell Block A, I shopped for criminals as I would for a new pair of jeans. *He might work, but I can do better. Okay fit, but not perfect.* Many of them were doing time for crimes I considered petty, and some of them were even innocent.

Every few cells, I'd pause to assess. Without fail, each time I peered in, the inmates met me in a brief face-to-face encounter at the barred doors. We looked into each other's eyes, and when they figured out my ability to see through them, some of them turned away. Others acted as private tour guides, proudly talking me through their lifetime of sins.

I worked my way to the wing where they housed Death Row inmates. They were on their way out anyway—I might as well get credit for them. A guard met me at the entrance. His nameplate read "J. Brooks."

"Sir, my name is Sergeant Starling, Clarice Starling." I waited to see if he'd laugh, but he remained expressionless. Because he bought the name, I made sure that's what he saw when he looked at my identification card. What he should have seen was "Reno Public Library," but instead he saw "Sgt. Starling: Alternative Placement Rehabilitation Coordinator" along with my picture.

"Sergeant Starling, I don't see you on today's visitor list." He flipped through several pages of names on his clipboard, and stroked his chin, sensing something was amiss.

"There I am." Using a freshly painted red nail, I pointed to the bottom of page four.

He shook his head, confused. "Sorry. Musta missed it."

Still hesitant to let me in, he clutched his key. "Alternative Placement Rehabilitation?" He snarled when he said "rehabilitation," as if, to him, no such thing ever happened.

I looked deep into his eyes and touched his hand. "Didn't you read the memo, Brooks? It's a new state-funded program. Let's call the chief warden. Maybe he forgot to get the word out." Brooks never read the warden's memos, and recently got written up for not staying abreast of policies and procedures.

"No, that's not necessary, ma'am." And with that, he unlocked the gate.

My heels clicked on the cement as I walked past five serial rapists, seven murderers, and one innocent man. I expected them to holler obscenities, but they just stared. I ordered Brooks to open cell 13, and I went in to talk to Jimmy Maxwell, wrongly accused of killing three little kids in a drive-by-shooting.

"Jimmy, I need some information," I whispered. "I'll tell you something, you tell me something." *Quid pro quo.*

"Why should I help you? Nobody's ever helped me."

I made sure he understood. "Do it for Shawn."

He stared at me, and I saw the name of his son, who he hadn't seen since the age of six months, tattooed into his dark forearm skin. "Who are you?"

"I'm going to get you out of here, Jimmy. I need to know the easiest way to get out to the back by the transportation lot."

Jimmy and I left together, along with twelve shackled inmates and one hypnotized prison guard. Five child molesters, all within days of being released from their three-year sentences, joined our group as we walked through the general population wing.

Two guards stood by the exit. Jimmy looked doubtful we'd get through. I worked the guards over so well, they escorted us to one of the activity vans and gave me the keys.

"I'll be right in front of you in my car, Jimmy," I said. "We're making one more stop about twenty minutes down the road. You know the deal—do this for me and you'll be free." I gave the van keys to him, and told the others to climb aboard.

Triple Homicide Ted was impatient. "Answer me, bitch. Where the fuck we going?"

"Ted," I answered, "it's a hot new program. You'll finally be rehabilitated."

By the time the guards recovered from their spell, we would be halfway to Reno. Their memories would fail them, and they'd think there'd been some sort of massive security breach. The video camera tape would look like the North Pole in a winter storm. Everyone would look for the missing convicts for the next decade, but they'd never find them. They were going to a different kind of jail.

Fifteen miles later, we came to our next destination: Meadow View Manor, a minimum security prison for white collar criminals. Jimmy stayed with the motley crew while I worked my magic inside on five inmates. I gave them the same story, but in order to convince a CEO who stole forty-seven of his employees' pensions, I had to promise him two things: access to a laptop to check his stocks, and the use of my cell phone.

Our criminal caravan drove back to my house for what the inmates assumed would be a briefing about the Alternative Placement Rehabilitation Program. We pulled into my driveway, and when Jimmy stepped out of the van, I asked him to meet me inside in a minute. Then, like a drum major in an orange jumpsuit parade, I herded twenty-two damned men through my threshold.

I directed the shackled, single-file line through my living room and into my kitchen, where I said I'd soon meet them. During the car ride home, it had occurred to me I had something Jimmy could use, so I grabbed it from under my kitchen table and delivered it to him as he waited for me by my front door.

"What's this?" he asked when I handed him a small, dark-green duffle bag.

Jimmy opened the bag and removed its contents: KKK Floyd's deep blue Wranglers, cheap tennis shoes, and button-down shirt. He'd left them at my appetizer party. At first, Jimmy's face scrunched up, but then, like a child opening a Christmas present, he looked at me and smiled.

I pointed to the orange uniform he'd worn for fifteen years. "Well," I said, "you won't make it to Mexico wearing that." I sent him to my bathroom to change into his new street clothes. A free man at last, he walked out holding up his old jumpsuit, folded to prison-inspection standards. The creases, perfect and crisp, were pretty enough to be on display at the Gap. When I glanced at his handiwork, he said, "Habit."

I handed him one hundred and eighty-two dollars and a piece of paper. "Sorry. It's all I have in my purse. Take the van to that address. A pretty woman will meet you there with a car and some new identification."

He relaxed his whole face and confessed, "I didn't do it."

For once, I looked deep into an innocent man's eyes. "I know."

"Are you some kind of angel?" Misty-eyed, Jimmy held out his hand.

I cupped it with both of mine, and gave him a hard squeeze. There was nothing to say but, "Good luck, Jimmy."

Halfway out the door, he turned around. "Not Mexico. Philadelphia—my son's in Philadelphia." And with that, he was gone.

I had to meet Luke at eight, so I promptly attended to the agitated men occupying my kitchen.

"Okay, gentlemen. I want you to think of your own detailed version of paradise. Go on, think about it. Be specific." One of them, who'd been resisting off and on, rolled his eyes. I shot him a telepathic peek at what I could do to his family, and in an instant, he conjured up his personal take on paradise—an island of half-naked teenage girls he had all to himself.

Precisely when they were feeling fully relaxed, I brought in Pluto, and he rounded the men up like the sheep they were. They descended my staircase with the final bit of false freedom they would ever sense. When the last scream drifted into a soft echo, I breathed a sigh of relief and left for my date with Luke.

When I walked into Duffy's, I saw Luke in a corner booth tugging at a rip in the seat's red vinyl. Duffy's was a local establishment known for its eclectic but low-brow clientele. I assumed it appealed to Luke because of its anonymity and flavor. In the back room, real pool players played real pool, and the CDs in the juke box hadn't been updated since 1981. Creedence Clearwater Revival and Peter Frampton were so overplayed, the numbers had worn off their selection buttons.

Behind the bar hung a painting just about anyone in Reno could describe. Once seen, it was hard to forget. Housed in a gold-leaf garage-sale frame, the woman stood nude, unashamed and beautiful. In complete contrast to the brassy-blonde beer poster girls who wore *Hee Haw* halters and posed on oiled-up Corvette hoods, the painting's Cherokee had untainted brown skin and young, natural breasts. Her gaze was the kind that whispered a personal secret to every onlooker, and what impressed me most was her ability to affect her viewers. People at the bar would notice her, become mesmerized, and temporarily forget where they were. She was sex, Old West, and mysticism, all rolled into one woman.

I got our drinks, then sat down next to Luke. He sipped his, and was surprised. "Wild Turkey. How'd you know what I drink?"

Rookie mistake. I was thinking like Tayanita. "Um, you mentioned it in class, that one day when you were yelling at us for not being interesting."

He laughed. "I didn't say you guys weren't interesting. I said that most of us aren't interesting enough to write about."

"How's the writing going? Doing much lately?"

He pointed to his bag under the table. "Just came from the library. Thought I could get something decent done there. Don't know. We'll see."

Note to self: Get into that bag.

"Hey. Weirdest thing came in the mail today." He took out a white envelope.

I mustered up a confused look. "What is it?"

"You'll never believe this. It's from *her.*"

The night I found out Luke went to high school with Venice Armada, I wrote Luke a Venice letter and forged her signature. In the letter, Venice told Luke she was writing a book about the hardships of growing up in a wealthy family, and needed some information about their high school escapades. His reply to Venice, which I also wrote and mailed, was a little more creative. If only I could have counted these two letters toward my writing class requirements.

"Yeah, she said I was the coolest guy in lame-ass high school and she always trusted me." I'd clearly appealed to his ego. He tapped the envelope on the table and sported a proud grin.

"Gonna call her?" I took a nonchalant sip of my drink.

"I can't believe it, but yeah, I think I will. She wants to talk with me, here in Reno of all places, to get material for her book." His finger circled the rim of his glass. "Wouldn't it be ironic if Poor Little Rich Girl, who's never written a damn thing in her life, publishes a book before I do?"

I mocked Venice without thinking. "Yeah," I said, "especially since you're the next," and I said this in a thick valley-girl accent, "like totally J.D. Frickin' Salinger."

"How did you know that? That was in her letter."

Shit, I did it again. "She, uh, said she liked Salinger in an interview I read awhile back."

That was true. I remember it because the magazine made a big deal over how her favorite book from high school was *Catcher in the Rye*, but when the interviewer made a joke about Holden Caulfield, she didn't get it.

"Well, she thinks I'll lend some sort of witty quality to her book. Said she remembers some poem I wrote as a sophomore. How embarrassing—I think it was about a porcupine."

I'd heard enough about Venice Armada. "Get over it," I said. "She's a blonde dimwit."

He scooted closer to me. "Do I sense a bit of jealousy, Miss Burns?"

"I'm just surprised you're so willing to see her." My long-shot of a plan had actually worked, but I worried it had worked too well.

"She's not my type at all, but something about what she said in the letter, the way she said it maybe, made me like her, made me want to help her."

I chuckled, and I could tell he wasn't sure why. I wanted to say, "I wrote the letter, dummy! It's me you like!" But I didn't. Instead, I thought of Venice, in some sort of designer halter top by a turquoise pool, reading her letter from me posing as Luke. Would a voice from the past affect someone like Venice Armada as it had Luke? I could handle her once she got to Reno, but my powers didn't work on the phone. I needed to see her in person, and I didn't have time to fly to Beverly Hills.

Luke headed for the men's room. "Be right back."

This was my chance. I took the disk out of his bag and put it in my purse. When he got back, he cleared his throat twice, which meant he was uncomfortable. "So, she wants to come this weekend. You're not gonna make me do this alone, are you?"

Thought he'd never ask. "Oh, I don't know. You're a big boy. Don't you want your little hottie to yourself?" I didn't want to seem like a girlfriend.

"I want *you* to myself." The two drinks had made him sound even more confident than usual.

"Well, since you put it that way . . ." I put my hand on his.

"I'll call you to let you know when she's coming," he said.

He put on his coat and left. I followed.

I had another date. Of sorts.

Chapter Twenty-Five

When I got to the Pompeii at 10 p.m., it was bustling with activity. When you're inside a casino, time all but stops. Whether it's sunny or rainy, night or day, what's happening outside the confines of the building is irrelevant. Everyone inside the mini-city of Pompeii was oblivious to the Christmas snowflakes collecting on the "Biggest Little City in the World" sign near the casino's front entrance.

Pompeiian regulars were lured by the chance to win the bright yellow Dodge Viper resting on a stage pedestal, or by alcohol, or by both, and it was this circus atmosphere I knew could work to my advantage.

On the escalator ride up to the second floor, I saw framed movie posters for *Adoring JC* and *Absolutely Adolf* hung on opposite walls. On the right side, a quote boasted, "*Adoring JC*, the story of a perfect man in an imperfect world." On the other side, I read contrary testimony: "*Absolutely Adolf* documents the origin of pure evil."

I glided upward, past both sides of the debate, and as I got closer to the top, it became clear to me that neither side was right. Members of both camps could beat each other to a pulp, but no winner would ever emerge until they could see the truth: Nobody is one-hundred percent *anything*.

I waded through a sea of gamblers carrying large plastic cups of coins, along with jumbo tumblers overflowing with Christmas drink concoctions, and made my way to Vesuvius Village. When I walked over to the Bestia, I saw them. They merged into the crowd, one by one, until I counted twenty-two. I could easily tell the difference between Peter's staff members and the regular Pompeii casino patrons. All of Peter's boys fidgeted like fourth-graders in the principal's office, and were, in general, pissed off.

Before I revealed myself, I watched them for a few minutes. Most of them smoked. Two of them had dressed up, hoping to look good for the boss. A couple of them talked about what the bonus might be. All of them wondered what Vesuvius Village had to do with it.

"It better not be a goddamned free pass to this shithole. We deserve a big fat check for making him so much fucking coin," said Ron, who was the kind of guy who, at the end of dinner, would calculate his portion of the bill down to the last penny. He threw his cigarette toward a display that showcased a mini-Mt. Vesuvius erupting with Christmas snow instead of molten lava. It was still smoldering when I walked up to greet them. By taking off my coat, I let them know, with slow, sultry motions, that I would be a special part of their bonus.

Donald, a type-A balding thirty-something, prided himself on being able to talk any elderly woman out of her savings, and dreamed of inheriting his boss's money-stealing dynasty someday. When he first saw me, he said to the guy next to him, "Piece of mother-fucking ass, dude."

Cathouse Kenny (*no explanation necessary*) whistled at me and made inappropriate gestures. Teddy was right. The real portal was powerful, and strong enough to make the whole scene plausible: beautiful girl shows up at a casino theme park to provide "services" to twenty-two men.

I saw their thoughts. Tommy Camp, the youngest of the swindlers, was lost in a fantasy involving an elaborate orgy scene on two of the roller coaster cars. I laughed.

Balding Donald approached me. "What's so funny, sweet cheeks?"

"Dessert first," I said, putting my lips around one of my special brownies. I took a big bite, then brought the rest of the brownie to his lips.

They were starting to draw attention to themselves, now that they'd gathered in a small group and were acting like perverts. Seeing a hooker in a casino was not that big a deal in Reno, but doing away with twenty-two people would require me to have the casino to myself. So I started a fire—no, not really. I just pulled the fire alarm. And I didn't really pull it. I willed a little boy named Stephen to pull it.

As panicked slot-players ran for the nearest exits, I made sure my victims were with me. *Really* with me. I generated as much energy as I could to keep them still. The casino visitors and most of the casino employees filed out into the snowy night, while we took cover under Teddy's lava stage beneath Mt. Vesuvius. We crouched down and waited until a security guard radioed the news: The park was empty.

We crawled out from under the volcano, and twenty-two zombies lined up for their dessert. I managed to feed them all without touching them, and eased the whole group over to the entrance of the Bestia.

Some dipshit in the back hollered, "Why are we lookin' at a roller coaster when we could be lookin' at your tits?!" They all yelled and applauded.

I put my finger to my mouth. "Shhh. Roller coasters excite me. Who wants to take a ride?"

They practically tripped over each other piling into the little cars. Once they were strapped in, I walked over to the control panel, which could turn an ordinary roller coaster ride into the ride from hell.

Once the lever was pulled, the cars would make their way to the designated spot, which was ten feet into the Porta Abyssus tunnel. The track would then disappear into thin air, and in a three-minute trip, the cars and their sinful cargo would reach their destination: a theme-park underworld no one knew about except people like me and Teddy. The coaster cars would make their way back, empty, and have just enough time to cool before regular operations could resume.

The thrill-seekers were eager to take their ride, so I opened the control panel door. There it was, just as Teddy had said—the little green door. It opened when I laid my palm down flat, and behind it was a red lever. How quaint—Christmas colors! I took one last look at the sorry band of thieves, now more somber than horny.

Here's to Grandma's retirement, assholes!

Task number one: *Check.*

Chapter Twenty-Six

I must have fallen asleep on the couch, because I awoke to a Christmas segment on a morning TV show. Strains of "The Christmas Song (Chestnuts Roasting on an Open Fire)" reminded me my ass would soon be roasting over an open fire of its own if I didn't complete my next two tasks mighty quick.

My Christmas calendar, a wooden frame with green and red cubes that counted down the days until Christmas, rested on my mantel. The frame had been a present from Ellen when she was twelve. She'd made it in industrial arts class, and gave it to me with a card that read, "Make Every Day Count—Santa's Coming Soon," except, as a joke, she'd transposed the letters to read "Satan." That stunt got her grounded for a week.

The cubes read "02." Two days weren't enough.

After I made coffee, I put in Luke's disk, and saw he'd written another chapter since I'd last read the manuscript.

Chapter Four

Thank God it was Friday. My writing was at a standstill and I needed my muse more than ever. I arrived at the bar to find Tayanita halfway through the legend of "How the Coyote Stole Fire." She looked different. Instead of her usual flowery peasant shirt, she wore a much more conservative white linen blouse.

I daintily placed my coffee cup down, flattered that Luke's fictional character was wearing my shirt. I kept reading.

One of the men said, "You should write modern-day versions of these stories—you know, throw in some inner-city shit. I bet you could make a killing. I'd buy 'em," and then he crashed his beer bottle into his buddy Fred's.

"Writing is harder than you think, Fred," Tayanita replied. Then, under her breath, she said, "A blank page is God's way of showing how hard it is to be God."

"That's my line!" I hollered at the computer, then reconsidered. I guess it was good news that Tayanita was exhibiting several of my attributes, because it meant Luke had been thinking of me.

He must have been thinking of the blurred lines between good and evil, too, because as Tayanita told the story of how the seemingly bad coyote stole the villager's flame, it became apparent he did so to avoid a terrible fire—a vision he'd had.

Tayanita had the ability to tell just the right story at just the right time. Her legends were sermons for her drunk congregation. At the end of Chapter Four, Jack, jealous that the old, smelly men had received positive attention from Tay while she ignored him, revealed that he was on to her. Her legends were all made up.

"So what?" she said.

"Why are you so nice to them?" he asked.

"They need me to be."

I was daydreaming about becoming his muse when I heard Luke talking on the answering machine.

"So, we're meeting Friday night, and I'd really like to see you. Hell, I'd like to see anyone. Anyway, Duffy's, seven-thirty."

Despite my rapidly approaching deadline, I spent the rest of the day helping Finn write a report. He had the day off from school, and Maggie had to go to the dentist and do a bunch of other errands.

"What's the report on, Finn?" I asked as we sat down at the computer table in their dining room, which was also in the midst of renovations. The floor was a bare sub-floor still waiting for carpet, so the acoustics made every noise doubly loud. David was out in the garage, and occasionally, we'd hear the buzz of a power saw or the banging of a hammer.

"Mrs. Williams said it could be about anything about tall tales." Finn poured a giant glass of juice for me into a Tyrannosaurus cup. "Legends, stuff like that. You know, Johnny Appleseed, Paul Bunyan. But I want to write about something cool that no one else will."

I took a drink of his juice. "How about Bigfoot?"

He slammed his hands down on the table. "That'd be so awesome, Lucy. Who's Bigfoot?"

He put his feet on my chair, and I pulled him closer to me.

I told him all I knew about the subject of Sasquatch.

"If there's nothing that shows he's real, why do so many people think he is?" Finn asked.

I resorted to tickling him, and making ape noises. "Because they like big monkeys!"

"No, really, Lucy," he said, giggling. "How come?"

"Well, why do people believe in Santa or the Easter Bunny?"

"Because they bring presents!" He paused. "But Bigfoot is big and scary and doesn't have candy or anything."

"Maybe people want to believe he exists, Finn, so they have something to wonder about—you know, something to search for."

"Like how Grandma Hoffman looks for shooting stars because she says it's God way of trying to talk to us?"

"Sure."

"I think nobody ever sees Bigfoot because he's so tired from protecting people, he has to sleep in a cave somewhere. I'm gonna put that in the end of my report. Mrs. Williams said we had to have a clusion—that's the end of the story. Do you like that clusion?"

"I love that *clusion*, Finn."

The next day, my calendar cubes read "01," and although I didn't want it to, the day flew by. Before I had a chance to get nervous about seeing Luke again, it was time to go meet him and Venice at Duffy's. It would be a tricky maneuver, keeping them from detecting my scheme.

When I walked in, I noticed they were in *our* booth. I was irritated, but needed to keep focused. I spied on them a little, which was easy because he couldn't see and she didn't know me. He was trying to look interested in the conversation, but by the way he stared into space, I could tell he was bored.

I touched his hand when I approached the table, and he greeted me with, "Hey, we just got here." He got up to give me a hug and a peck on the cheek, indicating I was not his sister, and I was glad. "Venice, this is Lucy Burns."

Venice was more Beverly Hills in person than on TV. Her hair was so bright blonde it cast a weird glow around her head. And she wore a cotton candy-pink tube top. It was designer expensive, but it was still a tube top. The hem of her miniskirt was so short it skimmed her pubic bone, and would've exposed pubic hair if she'd had any. She would be a natural Facilitator.

"Wow, I bet you're freezing! Nevada winters aren't like California's."

She tossed her hair and said in a surprised voice, "Yeah, it's really cold here." Luke looked my way and we both tried to keep from laughing. Her voice sounded like a kid who'd breathed an entire balloon's worth of helium, but more fake.

I was confused. "You sound a lot different on TV."

"Yeah, I use a voice double. My dad always makes them dub her voice over mine. He says it's a good idea. But he also thinks it's a good idea that I get a job!" A strange, high-pitched noise came out when she laughed.

When she attempted to scrunch her nose up, nothing happened. She'd had way too much fun with Botox in her spare time. Her face was expressionless. Whether she smiled, or whether she frowned, she looked the same. The only thing that actually moved was her hair and her tongue, and, sometimes, her eyes.

After a long silence, she spoke. "Well, I'm so sorry, Luke."

He looked puzzled.

I think she tried to smile. "You're such a little trouper."

Just then, someone sitting over at the bar hollered at Luke. For me, the interruption was more than opportune.

"Excuse me, ladies," Luke said. "I'll just be a sec."

While he was gone, I explained to Venice how Luke didn't want to talk about his illness, and to please not bring it up. In the letter, I'd told her he was dying—of "acute ennui." But he really wanted to see her again, while he could still walk.

I took her hand. "Your beauty has always been an inspiration to him, Venice." I looked into her aqua blue contacts. "You're his muse." She tried to push her bee-stung lower lip, taut with silicone, into a full pout, but it barely quivered. Both hands flew to her bulging tube top.

"I'm his muse? Oh my God! I've always wanted to be somebody's muse!" She watched Luke talking to someone at the bar, and shook her head. "He looks so . . . healthy. You know, except for the whole blind thing."

"I know. That's the frustrating part. He doesn't even look ill, does he?"

"How can I help?" she said.

"Well, he's under the illusion you're writing a book about high school—you know, the good old days." I whispered in her ear, "His meds are *very strong*."

"Should I just play along?"

"Exactly. For now, just pretend you're gathering information. Taking a trip down memory lane will be therapeutic for him. Maybe we could meet tomorrow morning for breakfast, and I could give you some things he wants you to have. High school stuff."

"Will Luke be coming?"

"No. He sleeps most of the day."

"Oh, duh. Like a dying man gets up at the crack of dawn!" She hit herself on her expressionless forehead.

Luke came back with more drinks. His new muse leaned into him and began musing. "Lukey, do you remember that Homecoming Dance, the one where I crashed my new Mercedes into that float?"

He chuckled. "Is that going in your book?"

She winked at me, then said to him in a slow, enunciated voice. "Yes. That's. Going. In. The. Book. I'm. Writing. About. High. School."

Luke looked in my direction and raised an eyebrow. She talked at him for an hour about the cheerleading squad, and asked several questions about some chemistry lab gone haywire, then said she had to get back to her hotel for a Power Pilates class.

After they said goodbye, I slipped her a note telling her when and where to meet me, then went home to invite someone else to the breakfast meeting.

"Lucy, is that you?"

"You know it's me. Why do you always do that?"

"Well, aren't *you* the little short-timer? I hate to tell you, but you've still got two major tasks to complete before your deadline, which is . . ." She apparently paused to look at her watch. ". . . in eighteen hours. Great. Interesting. Super. You're never going to make it."

"That's what I called about. Meet me for breakfast tomorrow, so I can introduce you to your new Facilitator."

She was silent.

For once, I had the upper hand. "Isn't a supervisor supposed to be excited about someone new to torture?"

"She better be trainable, or I'm not accepting her."

"Oh, she's trainable all right."

Chapter Twenty-Seven

The hotel restaurant smelled like cheese omelets and chocolate chip pancakes, and I have to admit, it smelled all the better because freedom seemed near. As Venice and I ate breakfast, she just sucked on ice chips and nibbled on dry toast. I changed the subject from Luke's misfortune to her dissatisfaction with life.

"Yeah, my dad's been riding my ass about getting a job, and giving back to the community, so I volunteered at a soup kitchen last week to shut him up."

"Good for you! How'd that go?"

She made an icky face—at least I think she did. "It was horrible. The cabbage soup was dreadful. And the people there really smelled."

"You know," I took a sip of my coffee, "I know about a job you'd really love."

Attempting sarcasm, she said, "A job *I'd* really love? Let's see, how about a job where I'd never get fat, and I'd never have to ask my parents for money? Oh, this is fun! How about a lifetime of credit at Betsey Johnson, and an unlimited supply of Ben & Jerry's?" She waited for my response.

"Sounds reasonable," I said.

Helium leaked from her lips. "Sounds too good to be true."

"That's just the thing, it's the perfect job for you. Think globally, Venice. You'd be able to give back to society, like your father wants you to do. My supervisor can explain the rest."

"Supervisor? I've always wanted a supervisor!"

"Just sign here, Venice."

"I want these to go away." She fingered some invisible wrinkles on her temple. "And I want a new car, and my own house with—"

I assured her, "You'll have all those things, and more," just as my supervisor walked in the door.

She walked over to our booth and reached her cold hand out to Venice, who shivered when she touched her. "This is her? Interesting. Great. Super."

"Just signed. She's all yours."

Venice warmed up with each new detail my supervisor revealed about the job. By the time she name-dropped Stella McCartney and explained how she could inquire about soliciting some custom pieces from her, Venice was sold, but said she didn't want to work in Reno—"too cold." My supervisor punched on her laptop. "No problem, Venus."

"*Venice*," said Venice, authoritatively correcting her.

"Right." With a few more clicks, she said, "How's Key West strike you?"

Task number two: *Check.*

Chapter Twenty-Eight

Only one song could reflect how fantastic I felt about completing the second task, so I cranked up "Weather the Storm," and celebrated with the man I always celebrate with.

I'd weathered the storm, but I hadn't made it through the entire deluge, so I couldn't help but feel a kinship with Teddy, the only other person I knew who'd beaten the unbeatable odds. I had but a few more hours to complete task number three, and it was time to find out who the "target" was. I walked to my mailbox to see if He'd sent the name, and out of nowhere, it magically appeared.

When I unfolded the paper, I couldn't believe my eyes.

Target: Matthew Finn Hoffman

I ran back in the house with the paper in my hand and began to frantically pace in my living room. How could this be? I thought, smashing one hand into another and practically hyperventilating. There must have been some sort of mistake! Finn was only eight! And my friend! We couldn't become adversaries overnight!

This was bad. This was so bad! My best friend's son is on the hit list to end all hit lists, and I'm the hit woman. I didn't want to hit anyone. I wanted it over.

When I finally cleared my mind, and winnowed my long list of questions to just a handful, I got out Teddy's business card and called him. To my surprise, he answered.

"Teddy, this is Lucy."

He heard my defeated tone and expressed his condolences. "Lucy, I thought I might be hearing from you. You sound stressed and angry."

"Why the hell is Finn the target?"

He was silent.

My heart hurt when I suddenly figured it out. "Targets aren't evil," I said. "They're good, aren't they, Teddy? Shit!"

I heard him sigh. "I told you this was going to be difficult."

"*Difficult?!* In order to save myself, I have to get rid of a perfectly innocent kid?!"

"Lucy," he said, his voice strong and steady. "Listen to me. You're not going to like this, but my advice to you is to let things run their course."

"That's your advice?" I screamed. "*Que sera sera?* 'Let things run their course'? You know what's at the end of the course for me? It's me losing everything." I mustered up some composure.

"Yes, there's a lot at stake. Do it or don't do it, but trust me: There are consequences either way."

I hung up on him. I'd never been good at having faith. Faith wasn't my thing. It was Ellen's.

After another hour of pacing and eight more cups of coffee, I decided to get some answers, so I ran next door.

Maggie was washing the breakfast dishes. "Hey!" she said. "I just made a pot of coffee. Whatcha up to?"

I sat down, hiding my shaky hands. "Maggie, do you ever go to church?"

"Church? You know I don't jive with organized religion. We were just talking about that last week, weren't we?" She took a bite of her toast. "I let Finn go with his friends sometimes, and every once in a while he goes to temple with David's mother. I think it's good for him to see different ways of doing things. Why do you ask?"

"Finn says prayers at night. Do you know that?"

"What's going on? You're sounding crazy."

"Nothing. I just think it's a little dangerous for him to be praying for things. I mean, prayers don't always get answered, and sometimes they're answered by the wrong people, and—"

She put her hands on my shoulders and gave me a mini-shake. "Lucy? Hello? Where's my normal friend Lucy? Finn's praying, or expressing his gratefulness, are hardly grounds to amp out."

"I'm sorry." She poured me a glass of juice. "Maggie," I said, taking her hand. "Now, please don't give me shit about this. Just answer, okay?"

She sat down, looking worried. "Okay."

"Has anyone ever . . ." I looked down because I knew how crazy I sounded. "Has anyone ever *contacted* you or Finn?"

Now she looked perplexed. "Anyone? *Contacted* me? About what?"

"I'm not sure." I began biting my nails.

"What the hell is wrong with you today, Lucy?"

"Okay. Has anyone ever told you you had any kind of special talents?"

"Well, there was this one guy."

I sat still in anticipation.

"He was a coffee-cup psychic. It's a type of psychic reading where they read your fortune by watching how the cream spirals in your coffee." She contorted her face into a pseudo-serious scrunch. "He told me I was destined to bring good into the world." She laughed and pointed a pencil at me as if it were a magic wand.

"Stop it, Maggie. I'm serious."

"So am I. You're not right today, Lucy."

"Where's Finn?"

"Where do you *think* he is? He's at school. It's the last day before break." She kept staring at me and poured me more juice. This was Maggie's way of making me better. In Maggie's world, there wasn't much that juice couldn't cure. Once, when Finn didn't feel well, she made him drink a whole gallon of juice in one sitting, and of course, he got sick.

"You teach him not to talk to strangers, right?"

"He doesn't jump in the back of vans when people offer him candy, if that's what you're asking. I want him to be safe, Lucy, but I don't want him going around thinking the world's a shitty place."

"Well, it is, Maggie. It's a shitty, horrible place, and Finn needs to watch his back."

"Okay, now you're scaring me. Is this about your damn job again? If you don't quit, I swear to God, I'll call your boss myself."

Without thinking, I grabbed her wrist. "Don't say that. Don't ever say that again."

"You're so polluted, Lucy. A spa day—that's what you need. Seaweed wrap, mud bath, the whole nine yards. Detox—that might do you good, too."

She had no idea how hard I was trying to rid myself of what was ailing me.

After I left Maggie's, I needed a pick-me-up, so I went to the private post office where Ellen's letters and notes got forwarded. It was in a strip mall next to the Little Bethlehem Book Store. The sky had turned gray and bleak, but I remained hopeful as I unlocked and opened the box.

For some reason, she'd stopped sending me letters about a year before, but I still checked the box once a month to see if there was anything new from her. And that day, I needed something from her more than ever. Things were grim. The only positive thing was that things couldn't get any worse.

When I looked in the mini-window of the mailbox door, I saw something beautiful—an envelope, made of familiar stationery, leaning on its side. I was so happy, I could hardly hold the key steady, but I did, and I opened the envelope with one giant rip.

> *Dear Lucy,*
>
> *I don't know if you'll get this. I don't know if you've gotten any of these. But you're my last hope. Lucy is very, very sick. She'll die soon if she doesn't get a kidney transplant. We've tried everything and everyone to find a suitable and willing donor. I'm relying on faith that you'll read this and call Mom so we can do some tests. They said an aunt could be the best match. There's no guarantee, but I just know you're the answer.*
>
> *Please, please, please call.*
>
> *Love,*
>
> *Ellen*

An invisible ghost must have clubbed me in the chest, because I couldn't breathe. The letter was postmarked a week ago, and the ache in the pit of my stomach returned. So that's why I hadn't heard from her for so long.

The whole way home, I couldn't stop thinking about the cruelty of fate. I'd left Ellen's life in order to save her, and now my very absence was threatening my namesake, little Lucy—the daughter who meant everything in the world to Ellen. I wanted to call my family right then, but I knew there'd be bad consequences all around so long as I was still working for Him.

Out of nowhere, I heard the sound of a ticking clock. I could see it in my head, too. It was a giant black and white clock, big enough to fill the whole sky, with a red second-hand moving much faster than it should, as if to say "you're screwed" with each passing nanosecond. I had only a few hours to do the impossible, and now more was at stake than *my* life. I had to win this battle in order to help Finn and Little Lucy retain theirs.

Chapter Twenty-Nine

1976

Nadia Comeneci earned the Olympics' first perfect score (a ten) in the 1976 Summer Games, and so Ellen decided to answer only to Nadia's name for all of June, July, and August. I answered to the name of the talented but less perfect Russian gymnast, Olga.

"Olga!" she'd say as she pointed her toes at our audience—thousands of blades of grass. "They're clapping for us."

But they weren't clapping for us. They were clapping for Ellen. Even Ellen's ponytail looked like Nadia's. That's one reason she got the privilege of being Nadia whenever we performed gymnastics in the front yard. The other was that Ellen was the better gymnast. She was the better everything.

It was a Saturday night when everyone realized Midnight, Ellen's kitten, was missing. Two days earlier, when I was six years old, I'd pretended to mail Midnight to our Aunt Edna, who, in my imagination, was coming soon for a visit.

At least that's the story I told everyone. Only I knew the truth—I did it to spite Ellen. Then, preoccupied by the excitement only spaghetti *and meatballs for lunch can ignite, I'd forgotten to take Midnight out of the land of the fake and return her to the land of the real.*

Midnight used up all nine lives sealed in a tomb of heat. When we made the draining trip to the backyard mailbox, during another of those scorching Indiana summers, we discovered the evil result of my original sin—a limp pile of bones and black-matted fur on a silver canvas of tin.

Years later, Ellen would laugh and call me by the nickname I used to hear in my sleep.

"Kitten-killer. Kitten-killer."

Chapter Thirty

Even my kitchen chair was cold and unforgiving. I sat with my pad of paper and realized my to-do list—all three items on it—was downright depressing.

1. Convince Pluto that the Main Office will have dog treats.
2. Stop lying to Pluto.
3. Lather both of us with extra lotion—our new home's high temperatures will be hard on our skin.

Just as I started to jot down item number four, the phone rang.

"Lucy?"

"What?!" I was in no mood to explain to a telemarketer why I wouldn't be needing any more long-distance minutes.

"*Someone's* gotta case of the crankies." Luke's jovial tone made me feel guilty. "Lucy Burns, I've got five words for you: impromptu picnic at my house."

This was officially the worst day of my life. "This is a really bad time, Luke."

"Okay. I can call back later. Hey, did you happen to see a disk fall out of my bag at Duffy's? I can't find it, and my manuscript—"

"Luke? I might have to go away." Even Pluto cried a little when I said this.

Luke's voice turned serious. "Lucy, what's the matter?"

I couldn't answer that question, so I asked one of my own. "In the history of the world, how many times has good triumphed over evil?"

"Define *evil*."

"Seriously, Luke, if you had to keep score, who do you think has more wins?"

"Do you want the happy answer or the *real* answer?"

"Real." I gulped.

"Evil. Without a doubt."

"That's what I thought."

"Hey, I'm on my way out," he said, "but I want to see you later."

Before I could tell him not to bother, I heard a dial tone.

I didn't want to do it, but it was time to remind myself why I was in such a predicament, so I walked into my bedroom, pulled the box from under my bed, and took out the black envelope, with the original letter—the one I hadn't read since I was ten. When I lifted the envelope flap and saw "To Whom It May Concern," I remembered having seen that phrase on a complaint letter my mother wrote to a department store for advertising the wrong sale items. But this was a different type of complaint letter.

To Whom It May Concern:

What I'm about to ask is between us. Just us. Ellen is really getting on my nerves.

Mother lets her do anything she wants, and she always bosses me around.

She is pretty and smart and good at everything. She is perfect. I hate her.

Please make her go away.

Sincerely,

Lucy Burns

My name had never looked so ugly. I waited for a slap across my face, a spanking, a lecture—anything to punish me for such a hateful act. But nothing happened. We just sat there—me, my letter, and my memories—hoping to be forgiven.

After an hour of sulking, I decided it was time to prepare Pluto and me for our inevitable journey, so I fed him, rubbed his ears, lathered on some lotion, and opened my journal file. When I was gone, I wanted Maggie, Ellen, and Luke to know the truth. My entry from a week ago looked so hopeful on the screen: "It's my turn to be saved, and the answer lies at the bottom of the Bestia."

The cursor blinked—as if to prompt me into action—but there was no action to take, at least none I could take in good conscience. I was ready to begin my very last journal entry when I heard the doorbell ring. It was Maggie and Finn.

Maggie looked to see if I had calmed down since this morning. "So, do you wanna come over tomorrow for a little Not-So-Christmas party?" she said. "Not-So-Christmas" is what David's mom called it. The in-laws celebrated Hanukah with David's sister, and spent Christmas with David, Maggie, and Finn, only they insisted on calling it Not-So-Christmas. Finn didn't really know why. He just knew there were plenty of presents.

"I don't think I can, Maggie."

Maggie stopped smiling. "Lucy, I don't like the sound of this."

"It's work. I have to move."

Her eyes welled up. "Oh, you've got to be kidding. You hate this job. You're going to just pick up and move wherever and whenever they want you to? You can't possibly be that passive, that servile."

Then, plopping on my couch, she broke down.

Finn looked frightened. "Mom? Are you crying?"

"No, honey, I'm fine." She wore a fake smile and sat down next to him at the table.

"Are you really moving, Lucy?" Finn asked. "Are you going to live near your sister?"

"I can't live near her, Finn."

Maggie now sat with her arms crossed, and told Finn to go into my office so she and I could talk in private. "Well, how long do you have to make up your mind?"

"It's made up, Maggie. I have to leave soon—maybe as early as tonight."

"Tonight?!" she yelled. "No, I need at least a week to talk you out of this."

"It's out of my hands, Maggie. Can't explain it. Just is."

"No, Lucy, that's where you're wrong. It's all up to you. Why can't you see that?"

I had to get out of there, so I walked to the door.

"So that's it, Lucy? You're just gonna leave me here sitting in your living room?"

I grabbed my coat. "Gotta go."

Given my imminent relocation, I wouldn't be able to return Luke's disk to him in person, so I went to the post office to drop it in the mail. On the way home, I heard a report on the radio. In my messed-up mind, it sounded like a one-act play.

BOB the Anchor: Breaking news from Riverdale Theatre. KLUV's Jane Mikolich is on the scene. Jane?

JANE the Reporter: Well, Bob, it's a grizzly scene here of biblical proportions. Apparently, it started with two different groups of protesters picketing *Adoring JC* and *Absolutely Adolf: What Were You Thinking?* They started arguing in front of the theater, and from there a full-blown riot exploded. Movie-going has never been this sinful. Bob, if you're looking for redemption, you won't find it here.

BOB: Could you describe the scene, Jane?

JANE: It's quite frightening, Bob. A gentleman by the name of—sir, would you tell us your name?

MAN in riot: Theo Foster. Get. Off. Me. Nazi-lover!

WOMAN in riot: Violence is not the answer!

JANE: I've got Matthew White here, Bob, who'd like to comment. What do you make of all this, Mr. White?

MATTHEW WHITE: Well, ma'am, I know it's just not Christian to see a movie as violent and profane as that Hitler movie.

JANE (with a tone rivaling Jane Fonda's in *The China Syndrome*): Do you think it glorifies the Holocaust, Mr. White? Do you think it exploits the victims of such a horrific crime? Is that why you and your group are here?

MATTHEW WHITE: I don't know how glorious or exploitatious it is, or whatever you said, cuz I haven't seen it, but I hear it has like ten "F" words and about five-thousand on-screen deaths. Now, folks just don't need to see that kinda thing. I mean, we're pretty certain people actually died in that Holocaust, but no one really knows for sure.

JANE: I believe it was six million people, Mr. White. [Microphone thumps.] Ma'am? Uh, Bob, this is—

GIRL in riot: I'm Annie. Look, *Absolutely Adolf* is a dark comedy . . . these morons aren't getting the joke!

JANE (grappling with microphone): Mr. White? Sir, please stop grabbing my microphone—

BOB: Jane? Are you there? . . . That was Jane Mikolich . . .

When I pulled into my driveway, I could sense something was amiss. I heard the phone ring just as I walked through my front door. Maggie was out of breath. "Lucy, have you seen Finn?"

"What do you mean? He was with you when I left."

Her sentences ran together. "He was really upset when we left your house, and about an hour after we got home, he just disappeared. I thought he was playing in his room, but when I checked on him, all I found was his God's Eye with a note to you underneath it.

"What did it say?" I said.

"'Dear Lucy,'" Maggie read, "'I know the answer and I want to help save you. Please don't go anywhere before I get back.'"

When I heard the word "save," a sharp pain shot through my chest. He must have seen the journal entry on my computer screen, the one that read: "It's my turn to be saved, and the answer lies at the bottom of the Bestia."

"Oh my God."

"What?! Why 'Oh my God,' Lucy?"

But before Maggie had time to come over, I was gone.

Chapter Thirty-One

My cell phone rang on my way downtown to Vesuvius Village. "Lucy? Venice and I are having a great time. She's a gem. Just great. Super." Then she whispered, "Perfectly naïve. Good work!"

"Go away."

"Funny, because that's what I called to tell you—it looks like you'll be going away for a while. You almost made it, Lucy. I'm impressed. But I knew you were weak. Off to help a friend, huh?"

I hated how she knew everything.

"All you have to do is let him go, Lucy, and you'll be free—you'll get what you want. Now, I don't really care either way, but I wanted to make sure you knew what you were doing. Oh, hope you don't mind, but I gave him a little help getting to his destination."

"Don't you touch him! Make sure nothing happens to him."

"Then I guess something's going to happen to you."

I was slow and deliberate. "Stay away from both of us."

"Settle down, Lucy. I'm busy familiarizing Venice with her new toys. Anyhew, I've heard great things about the Main Office." She cackled. "Kidding, kid. It's a living nightmare."

Just as I hung up, my car started to chug. I looked at my dash, and my gas gauge was suddenly and inexplicably dipping into the red. I ran a block to the nearest gas station, and on the way back, gusts of wind and blowing snow created an instant blizzard. I'd finished putting in three gallons when I heard a loud crack. The tree next to the road now rested on my car's hood in a bed of mangled metal.

They weren't exactly playing fair.

There was no time to wait for a ride, so I ran the rest of the way. I scampered through a parking lot full of Christmas gamblers. The sky was now a dark mess of swirling clouds. I sprinted through the entrance, past the blackjack and craps tables, and stopped when I got to Vesuvius Village.

I thought I saw Finn behind the fence surrounding the Bestia, but when I got closer, all I saw was his puffy green coat, lying amidst old wood and garbage. His canvas school bag was tipped over, his crayons and books spilled onto the ground.

"Finn?!" I turned my head and hollered into the crowd, but I knew he wasn't out there. I went over to the tunnel entrance, saw two discarded boards, and remembered how Teddy had described it. "The portal has two exit points. One is accessed by riding the roller coaster. The other can be accessed by foot."

"No," I said.

The tunnel entrance was shaped like a dog, and above two angry dog ears, a sign read "*Cave Canem.*" "Beware of the dog" was probably sound advice, but I had a feeling a dog was the last thing I needed to worry about. The roller coaster cars weren't due for another minute, so I followed the steel track into the tunnel, where I saw Finn's gloves lying near a hole. It was dark, but there were patches of light creeping in.

I ripped up the remaining boards and heard a familiar sound. I'd heard it two nights earlier after the men's screaming had subsided and the roller coaster had come to a halt. A strange sucking sound came from the darkness. After squeezing my hips through the small opening, and dangling my feet for a moment, I let go of the top boards. When I fell several feet, I hit bottom. The vacuum sound crescendoed into a loud hiss.

In complete blackness, I waved my hands, hoping to feel something—anything. I put my fingertips on my face to make sure I was still there, then began inching my way forward with outstretched arms. Whatever was underneath my feet felt like sand and gravel at first, but gradually turned mushy, until each step was sticky with some sort of sludge.

I'd been stumbling in blackness for a long time when I put my arms down for a rest. A few seconds later, I felt something warm and gummy on my forehead. It reeked like week-old road kill, and I realized I'd smelled that odor before—Ellen's kitten Midnight had produced the same knee-locking stench after baking and decaying in the mailbox for three days.

I moved my hands enough to know that the space I'd been walking through had shrunk to half its size, both in height and width, so I crawled through the muck for several minutes more.

"Finn?!" I called in the darkness.

No answer. But a new sensation came over me—an indescribable sense of suffering, like the fleeting feeling one has right before the phone rings with bad news. But it was a constant ache, an oppressive sixth sense I didn't want to possess. The feeling got so uncomfortable, I stopped to listen for moans or screams, but heard only the swooshing of air and my own labored breathing.

Then the hissing stopped, and it got really, really hot. The damp air took on a smell so strong, it was if I was breathing in musty, dug-up soil. Beads of sweat clung to my face and jiggled with each crawl through the dense waves of heat.

When I swiped at my sweat-drenched brow, I noticed I now had more room to move. I kicked my legs out and realized the tunnel I'd been in had expanded, but it wasn't until I stood up and walked in a circle that I saw the light—not so much a light as a twinkle.

It was far in the distance, and each time it flickered, I walked faster. As I moved closer to it, the air got cooler, and the aching sensation in my belly subsided. When I looked down and saw my feet for the first time in about an hour, I heard two faint voices.

I came to an opening that at first glance seemed to be a room, except it had no ceiling, walls, or doors. It looked like a painting whose edges had been erased or made fuzzy, and the only things in focus were the table and chairs where Finn and a man now sat.

The table, made from a giant slab of mahogany polished to a shiny luster, rested on thick, ornately carved legs, and the wooden chairs were upholstered in a red, Asian-inspired silk fabric.

The man was in his early forties but seemed older. Everything about him looked rich and perfect—his black tailored smoking jacket, his Mont Blanc quill pen, and his luxurious pad of parchment paper. His hands were freshly manicured and, to my surprise, he was clean-shaven. But unlike the rest of him, his hair was an untidy collection of long gray curls uncontainable by any hair gel.

Finn and the man took turns putting coins in an antique gumball machine on the table and watching the multitude of colored gumballs reshuffle in the see-through bulb. Next to the table sat a vintage pinball machine featuring the original Charlie's Angels in their famous silhouetted trinity of hair, jumpsuits, and guns. Hanging on invisible walls were two movie posters: *The Good, the Bad and the Ugly* and *Willy Wonka & the Chocolate Factory*.

The man lit his pipe. "How fortunate for you, Finnegan. You get to go first."

"Smoking is bad for you," Finn said, looking back at the game board. "Do I get something special for going first?" I could barely hear him, but it *was* Finn.

There was a condescending snicker. "Yes, Finnegan. You get a double word score. Haven't you ever played before?"

"Lucy was going to teach me next time she babysat. Do you know Lucy?"

The voice got clearer as I walked closer. "Yes, I know Lucille. So how is she these days?"

Finn put down a "Q" on the center pink star, then followed with an

"A" and a "T" and said, "Lucy needs help."

"Yes," He answered. "She certainly does." Then He looked at Finn and folded his hands. "Hmmm, 'Qat.' An evergreen shrub. It seems you've played before."

Finn smirked. "Maybe a few times." He counted up the tiles. "Let's see, that's twelve. Times two. Equals twenty-four."

"Right." When He unhurriedly recorded the score, it was in perfectly neat numbers, written with the flair of a calligraphy artist.

The man looked into the darkness where I stood. "Are you going to join us, Lucille, or are you just going to stand there looking dumbfounded?"

Chapter Thirty-Two

Finn turned around casually and gave me a bright smile. "Lucy! Wanna play? This is my friend Bernard."

"Please, Finnegan," He said in a smoldering voice, "Bernie."

Breathless, scared, and determined, I took a step toward the pair at the table. Bernie placed his next word on the board and said, "Before you come rushing in, Lucy, think this through. Let him stay and you'll be free. Isn't that what you want—to be free to live your life? He's already here, you know." He stared at me with anticipation. "Just turn around and walk out."

I looked at Finn. "I came here for him. He's leaving. I'm staying. Get up, Finn."

"Bernie" stared at the game board and avoided looking at me, then attempted to smooth his disobedient hair several times, but it remained unruly. He cleared his raspy throat and displayed a facial expression that indicated things were about to escalate. Still gazing at the board, He signaled for me to leave by raising his hand in an exasperated gesture. "Good day, Lucille."

"Finn, get up and walk out the door," I said.

"The reason poor Finnegan is here in the first place is because of you, sweet Lucille." Bernie looked straight at me. "Honestly, Lucille, do you think you didn't know what would happen after you made that little journal entry on your computer? You were secretly hoping Finnegan would find it—"

"No!"

". . . so you could wash your hands of the whole situation. And what do you know? Your *prayers* were answered. You had better be careful what you wish for, darling. Your wishes always seem to get someone hurt." He picked his teeth. "Poor Ellen. All those years ago, run down by that big red truck—the truck *you* sent, Lucille."

"Finn, get out of here!" I yelled. Finn looked nervous and confused.

"Stay there, Finnegan. She doesn't really mean that. Lucille, you are free to go. Forget you were even here. There is no need to put on a big show. After all, this boy is only a *neighbor*. He's not even family. And Lord knows what you do to family." Bernie pulled his hand across his throat. It broke my heart thinking what most likely would happen to little Lucy without my help.

"Stop!" I said.

"Poor, sweet Ellen. You know, she actually saw that truck coming. She jumped in front of it to protect you." He smiled. "If that isn't irony, I'll eat my pitchfork."

"I've made my decision! I'm staying!" I moved to grab Finn.

"And was it also your decision to obliterate everything good that's ever happened to you?" He reached into the air and magically yanked down a white screen showing me on my fifth birthday. It was secret footage of my first atrocity. "See that fragile little robin's egg you found in your backyard? Such a beautiful blue, isn't it, Lucille? Wait. Here's my favorite part. Let's watch!"

Suddenly, we were all sitting in squeaky theatre seats devouring popcorn from big tubs. "Finnegan," He said with raised eyebrows. He pointed to the screen, which showed me hiding in my childhood bedroom, pretending to be a mother bird. He shook his head in disgust. "Look, no innate mothering abilities," He said as I placed a pillow on the egg and sat on it.

"I was trying to help it hatch!" I yelled.

Finn asked, "Why are you squishing the bird's egg, Lucy?"

"You see, Finnegan, Lucille's idea of nurturing usually results in disaster." He snapped his fingers. "See Exhibit B." The footage, now with scratchy, distorted audio, documented a series of deaths in fast-forward. A limp canary in a lonely cage. A bellied-up goldfish. A heat-baked kitten.

"Stop it!" I screamed.

"Oh, don't you think this is pertinent information for your new boy-friend, Lucille? You had to pick a blind man because you don't want him to see who you really are, isn't that right? And the thought of *you* having a baby? Please. You can't keep a fungus alive." The tape reel spun out of control. "See. It never ends, Lucille. Your whole life has been a disaster, and it was one long before I came along. Face it. You are an empty, selfish shell of a woman, and Finn is better off without you!"

Just then, Bernie's eyes turned a wild red, and a blast of air knocked me off my feet. I landed on my back, but when I lifted up my head to get my bearings, He was directly above me. Only it wasn't Him any-more. It was a horrific, horned creature, the kind of monster that makes a nightmare a nightmare.

A non-human voice boomed, "LEAVE!"

Another strong gust of hot air knocked me off my feet, and this time pushed me toward the exit. I dug my fingers into the ground but couldn't get a grip. The opening stood behind me. Faster and faster, I was blown toward it. Just then, I wrapped both arms, pretzel style, around the front leg of the pinball machine.

As I held on, the fiery wind burned my hands and face. With His bulging, leathery body raging in front of me, the doorway behind me, and Charlie's Angels at my side, I screamed, "I'm staying!" I looked at Finn, and managed to cry and whisper at the same time. "He's good. He is perfect."

And as quickly as it came, it left. Everything stopped. The wind. The flames. In fact, the room looked normal. I was baffled by what I saw.

As if nothing ever happened, Finn sat at the table unaffected.

Bernie, still in his smoking jacket, placed his pipe on the table, closed his eyes, and with a half-smirk, said, "Well, I'll be damned."

I didn't know what was going on, but I felt myself gaining strength, so I walked over to Finn and pulled him close to me. I hugged him hard and kissed his cheek again and again.

Finn was confused. "What's going on, Lucy?"

"Finnster," I said, wiping tears from my cheeks. "I need you to be brave. Walk out that door and run home, okay?"

There was a long pause.

"So shines a good deed in a weary world," said Bernie. "Why don't you show him yourself, Lucille?"

"What game are you playing now, you bastard?" I said.

"Ouch. I miss the good old days when you referred to me as 'To Whom It May Concern.' What happened to us, Lucille?" Bernie wore a frown. He put another dime in the gumball machine and looked disappointed when a white one came out. "I was really looking forward to spending time with one of you. There's nobody here worth talking to. Everybody is such a downer." He popped the white gumball into his mouth.

I looked straight into His gleaming eyes. "What are you saying?"

"I'm saying that you passed." He got up from his chair and walked over to Finn and me.

I stared at Bernie in disbelief.

"Go ahead. I know you want to check." From behind his back, he pulled a shiny mirror, the kind I'd heard about in fairy tales, and held it in front of me. "Look. Feel around for it, if you want. It's gone. You're no longer bound to me."

For fifteen years, I'd seen a silver "F" stare back at me when I looked in the mirror, but all I saw now was my bare skin. My shaking hands felt for my neck, and indeed nothing else was there.

Finn looked at me with fearful eyes. "What's going on, Lucy? I don't want to leave without you."

"You won't have to, Finnegan. Lucille here passed the test."

"What kind of test? I got an A-plus on my multiple choice last week," Finn said.

"In a way, this was multiple choice, too. Only Lucille didn't get to know all the options ahead of time." Bernie walked back to the table, put away the game board letters, and smiled wryly. "You picked a fine time to leave me, Lucille."

"So we can leave—just like that?" I asked as Bernie put the game board away. "This just doesn't fit your . . ."

He sensed my skepticism, so He reached into space, and from nowhere pulled down a miniature statue featuring the goddess Astraea draped in a toga-style sheet, holding the Scales of Justice in one hand and a sword in the other.

Bernie held the statue in the palm of his hand and touched it as you would a baby animal. "It's a delicate balance, Lucille." He placed his manicured index finger on one end of the scale and made it drop with a clink. "Extremes of any kind create imbalance."

With another finger, he weighted down the scale's other end. "Good and evil cannot exist separately, because they are mutually dependent." He paused. "A functioning symbiosis." He stared through his invisible wall, and in a dreamy ponder, said, "Yin and Yang. Beowulf and Grendel. Superman and Lex Luthor. You can't have one without the other."

I thought of the little girl in my painting, and said, "Light . . ."

". . . and shadow." Bernie sat down in his chair and leaned back. "They come from the same place, Lucille—light and shadow. A shadow is merely the *absence* of light." His pause indicated he was letting his guard down. "After all, when all's said and done, who do you think I really work for?" He pointed a finger upward.

Just then, something else occurred to me. I thought of Teddy's horoscope—"Give and you shall receive."

"Then Teddy must have passed the test, too!" I said. I was relieved to learn Teddy hadn't damned an innocent target.

"Of course, kid. He's Teddy Nightingale. Ever heard a little lyrical masterpiece called 'Boogie with a Capital B'?"

It was true. Teddy had fans everywhere.

Epilogue

When I looked in Maggie's bathroom mirror, I saw the spidery beginning of a wrinkle near the corner of my left eye, and almost shed a tear of joy. My skin had an opaque finish—the kind a car has when it needs buffing—and my eyes, puffy and a bit tired, didn't look as bright as they used to. They just looked like other women's. I was imperfect. And beautiful. Halfway down the full-length mirror, I paused at my mid-section, which was swollen to ridiculous proportions.

I turned to the side and witnessed a profile that looked like an erect sway-back horse—my curves were so drastic, it made me question whether my spine could handle any more torque. My holiday outfit, a clingy little black dress from a trendy maternity boutique, was two sizes too small. I made no effort to hide the life growing inside of me—I didn't want to.

I wore Finn's Christmas present, a candy cane necklace, as if it were an emblem representing my new self.

Luke waited for me in the hallway. He'd started doing that soon after I became pregnant. Because he couldn't see me, or the baby, he said he wanted to be near us all the time. I walked out of the bathroom, forgetting he would be standing there, and my belly torpedoed into him while my heel crushed the top of his foot.

He winced in pain, and carried on too long, making me fold my arms and feel like Shamu, but I didn't complain. I had waited a long time to look like Shamu.

"You're folding your arms, aren't you?" Luke said, reaching for me and my big belly. "Hold out your hands." He handed me a bound ream of paper tied with my red silk scarf, and apologized. "Couldn't find the wrapping stuff."

I untied it, and saw *The Legend of the Corn Maiden*, by Luke Marshall. When I flipped to the next page, it said, "For Lucy, my 24-hour muse."

A warm sensation shot through me and I placed my hand, open-palmed, on my stomach out of nervous habit. "No chocolate?" I said.

"No," he smiled. "Just this."

My voice broke a little when I touched his face. "I love it."

We walked downstairs to find everyone sitting around the giant, farmhouse-style table, which was decorated with red dishes, white linens, and one flickering green candle placed in the center. There were no traces of the old kitchen. A wall had been knocked out to make room for the breakfast nook area, the place where many future gatherings would take place. One side of the nook was a floor-to-ceiling chalkboard, and I saw remnants of old Scrabble games and homework problems.

From the table, Maggie viewed her gourmet kitchen, complete with honey pine cabinets, stamped tin ceiling, and granite countertops. A large and regal copper hood jutted down from above the high-tech range, looking like a divine, upside-down megaphone—a direct line to the Almighty himself. The whole house smelled like hot cinnamon rolls, coffee, and Christmas trees.

I leaned over and put my arm around David. "Kitchen looks great," I said. David had finally completed all his projects and it was time to celebrate.

He poured some juice into a fancy glass, and announced a toast. "Happy Not-So-Christmas brunch, everybody."

Next to David sat Maggie. She was thrilled to have everyone there, but she didn't want to seem affected. She turned to me, smiled, then held up a basket. "Another roll, fat-ass?"

I laughed and asked Finn to pass the basket. Finn sat next to

Squeaky, which worked out great because when seated, their eyes were at the same level. Squeaky looked festive in his holiday gear—a red and green T-shirt that showed Santa washing his sleigh, singing, "Ho-Ho-Hose that car off at Snow White's Car Wash."

Squeaky folded his hands, and said, "Uh, before we eat this fine meal, I want to give you guys a little something," then handed everyone but me a small white envelope with a coupon for one free car wash. He handed me something under the table and winked. "It's for after the baby."

I scooted my chair out a bit, so I could see past my bulge, skimming the underside of the table. While everyone else ate and passed around waffles and bacon, I snuck a peek at my gift from Squeaky. It was a bright purple T-shirt that read, "I Came Clean at Snow White Car Wash."

A healthy and happy Little Lucy snuck up behind my chair and tapped my shoulder. I swung my belly around to greet her, because I knew what she wanted. She tucked her silky hair behind her ears, widened her brown eyes, and put her hands on me.

"Next Christmas," she whispered, "can I sit by the baby?"

I held up my pinky and interlocked it with hers.

"I promise," I said.

And there sat Ellen, too. During the height of commotion and conversation, I caught her staring at me from the end of the table. When I stared back, for just a moment, I saw myself. This happens sometimes with sisters.

And then I thought of me and Ellen in our leotards, cartwheeling our way across a sea of grass, making promises against the backdrop of a pink Indiana sky.

Together.

Without saying a word, we celebrated the first day of forever. And all was as it should be—as promised.

Acknowledgments

A huge thank you to everyone at Bancroft Press for making this book possible. My agent and publisher, Bruce Bortz, tirelessly fought for this story, and took a chance on a little writer from Nevada. For that, I am eternally grateful. And to Harrison Demchick, editor extraordinaire, thank you for seeing the things I didn't, and for making everything I do better.

Thank you to Heidi, Angie, Danielle, Meg, Monica, Barbara, Zoe, and Steph, my loyal manuscript readers and personal cheerleaders.

Thank you to Ben Rogers for his thoughtful feedback on *Lucy*'s early drafts.

Thanks to my photographer, Matt Theilen, for my book jacket photo.

A big thanks to Mark Leiknes, artist and brother-in-law, for creating the coolest book cover ever!

Thank you, Jane Green, for your generous words and willingness to support a new writer.

Thank you to my friends Mena and Adam for loving *Lucy* from the beginning, and for sharing her with Turkey and the rest of the world.

Thank you to Lorna for being a valued reader and friend, and to Scott for helping me celebrate *Lucy*'s arrival in style.

To all my family, especially Diana, Denise, and Leah for your patience and support during the writing of this book.

To Matt Jimenez and Randy Foster, who went beyond the call of duty as brothers-in-law—you are truly invaluable readers.

Thank you, Mom, for praising the first, bad story I ever wrote.

And to Susan, thank you for your astute revisions on draft number one (*there's a dog in this book?*), but mostly for being my ideal reader and my ideal friend.

Most of all, a heartfelt thank you to my husband, John, for helping me turn a little story into a big dream. Thanks for reading and fixing scores of drafts (no hyperbole this time) and being my first editor when no one else would have me. Really, you created *Lucy*, and I filled in the blanks. Thank you. On every single page of this book, in some way, you are there.

About the Author

Elizabeth Leiknes grew up in rural Iowa and can make thirty-seven different dishes featuring corn. She attended The University of Iowa as an undergrad, and The University of Nevada, Reno for her Masters.

Her most recent accomplishments include publishing an article entitled "Writing Spaces: Expanding the One Story House" in *The Quarterly*, and completing two other novels, *Black-Eyed Susan*, and *The Understory*.

Lucy Burns was "born" somewhere between a third and fourth helping of Captain Crunch during Elizabeth's sixth month of pregnancy with her first child, but the majority of Lucy's story was written during her maternity leave, somewhere between debilitating bouts of new-mother panic attacks, and squirting milk in various inappropriate locations about town.

Elizabeth has a love/hate relationship with great white sharks, and a slight penchant for speaking in hyperbole, which she says she *never* does.

She now lives and teaches English near Lake Tahoe with her husband, two sons, and mentally ill cat.